OCT 1 4 2025

Twice

Also by Mitch Albom

The Little Liar

The Stranger in the Lifeboat

Finding Chika

The Next Person You Meet in Heaven

The Magic Strings of Frankie Presto

The First Phone Call from Heaven

The Time Keeper

Have a Little Faith

For One More Day

The Five People You Meet in Heaven

Tuesdays with Morrie

Twice

A NOVEL

Mitch Albom

WILLARD LIBRARY
7 W. VanBuren St.
Battle Creek, MI 49017

HARPER

An Imprint of HarperCollins*Publishers*

TRY ME
Words and Music by JAMES BROWN
© 1958 (Renewed) WARNER-TAMERLANE PUBLISHING CORP.
All Rights Reserved
Used by Permission of ALFRED MUSIC

MAKE SOMEONE HAPPY
Lyrics by BETTY COMDEN and ADOLPH GREEN Music by JULE STYNE
© 1960 STRATFORD MUSIC CORPORATION
All Rights Administered by CHAPPELL & CO., INC.
All Rights Reserved
Used by Permission of ALFRED MUSIC

Without limiting the exclusive rights of any author, contributor, or the publisher of this publication, any unauthorized use of this publication to train generative artificial intelligence (AI) technologies is expressly prohibited. HarperCollins also exercise their rights under Article 4(3) of the Digital Single Market Directive 2019/790 and expressly reserve this publication from the text and data mining exception.

This is a work of fiction. Names, characters, places, and incidents are products of the author's imagination or are used fictitiously and are not to be construed as real. Any resemblance to actual events, locales, organizations, or persons, living or dead, is entirely coincidental.

TWICE. Copyright © 2025 by ASOP, Inc. All rights reserved. Printed in the United States of America. No part of this book may be used or reproduced in any manner whatsoever without written permission except in the case of brief quotations embodied in critical articles and reviews. For information, address HarperCollins Publishers, 195 Broadway, New York, NY 10007. In Europe, HarperCollins Publishers, Macken House, 39/40 Mayor Street Upper, Dublin 1, D01 C9W8, Ireland.

HarperCollins books may be purchased for educational, business, or sales promotional use. For information, please email the Special Markets Department at SPsales@harpercollins.com.

hc.com

FIRST EDITION

Library of Congress Cataloging-in-Publication Data
Names: Albom, Mitch, 1958– author
Title: Twice: a novel / Mitch Albom.
Description: First edition. | New York, NY: Harper, an imprint of HarperCollins Publishers, 2025
Identifiers: LCCN 2025027979 (print) | LCCN 2025027980 (ebook) | ISBN 9780062406682 hardcover | ISBN 9780062406705 ebook
Subjects: LCGFT: Magical realist fiction | Novels | Fiction
Classification: LCC PS3601.L335 T87 2025 (print) | LCC PS3601.L335 (ebook)
LC record available at https://lccn.loc.gov/2025027979
LC ebook record available at https://lccn.loc.gov/2025027980

25 26 27 28 29 LBC 5 4 3 2 1

For Janine, and the loving life she has given us

You can't go back and change the beginning, but you can start where you are and change the ending.

—C. S. LEWIS

Twice

Prologue

August 1978

They were calling it "the storm of the year." All along Market Street in the city of Philadelphia the rain blew sideways and the wind gusted near hurricane force. Buses splashed through huge puddles and thunder rumbled overhead.

In the middle of this chaos, a woman suddenly appeared, young, not yet twenty years old. Her thick hair, the color of coal, blew wildly around her face, covering her eyes. She seemed confused, as if this storm were a surprise.

She clutched her handbag and undid the clasp as the rain soaked her jeans and matted them against her legs. She pulled out a small object, stared at it, then slowly put it back.

Looking up, she spotted the front entrance of Gimbels department store. She narrowed her gaze at the sight of a revolving door, and a young man at the window, waving his arms.

A breath caught in her chest. She shivered slightly, then began to walk toward him, steadily, deliberately, as if she had been here before.

One

NASSAU, BAHAMAS
FORTY YEARS LATER

The detective clucked his tongue. He stared at the gray-haired man slumped across the table.

"Come on, friend. How did you do it?"

Silence.

"We can sit here all day if that's what you want to do. Is that what you want to do? Sit here all day?"

The small room inside the police station was hot and in need of paint. The only furniture was a wooden table and the two occupied chairs. The detective, Vincent LaPorta, opened a roll of hard candy, plucked the top one out, cherry red, and popped it in his mouth.

"Want one?"

The man snorted a laugh.

"What's so funny?"

"The name."

"Life Savers?"

"Yes."

"Wish you had one now?"

"My life's been saved too many times already."

LaPorta waited for more, but the suspect hooked his fingers and looked down, as if praying. His face was tanned and unshaven, his jaw and cheekbones well-defined, maybe too defined, like a man who'd grown thin from an illness.

His mustard-colored shirt and navy-blue pants were badly wrinkled, as if he'd slept in them.

"Let's go over the accusation against you," LaPorta said. "Maybe it will jog your memory."

He slid a photograph across the table.

"In a single visit, at the island's largest casino, you correctly played three straight roulette numbers, winning over two million dollars. Then you walked out the door."

"Is that a crime?"

"No, but only because we haven't pieced together how you did it."

"So, not a crime?"

"Look, friend. My job is catching casino cheats. I've been doing it a long time. Vegas. Atlantic City. Now here in the Bahamas. What you did, you can't do without breaking the law."

"I see." The man nodded thoughtfully. "May I ask you a question, Detective?"

"Go ahead."

"Why this kind of work?"

"What are you, a shrink?"

"Just curious."

LaPorta smirked. "Let's just say I don't like people who bend the rules."

"Ah. Then you wouldn't like me."

LaPorta studied his tall, rangy suspect, who wore a small earring on his left lobe and no socks under his weathered loafers. LaPorta guessed he was in his late fifties and not particularly well-off. In that way, he was like any number of men you'd find placing bets at an island casino. But his attitude under interrogation was unusual. Normally, suspects were jumpy, perspiring, answering too quickly or too slowly. This man almost seemed *bored*.

"Come on. Tell me how you did it. You got an inside guy?"

"I've committed no crime."

"Three straight roulette numbers? You don't call that *suspicious*?"

"Suspicion and belief can't share the same bed."

"What's that supposed to mean?"

"It means if I told you the truth, you'd have to accept something you can't."

"Try me."

The man squinted. "No."

"You realize cheating a casino can get you sent to jail?"

"Yes."

"For a long time."

"Time doesn't mean much to me."

"Why not?"

"It's complicated."

LaPorta bit down on his hard candy.

"Tell me about a woman named Gianna Rule."

The man's expression changed. LaPorta perked up. *Here we go. Stay with this.*

"You went to a bank after you won that money and you wired it to a Gianna Rule. We can find her. Bring her in. Maybe charge her as a coconspirator. Is that what you want?"

The man blinked. LaPorta leaned across the table.

"Like I said: try me."

"All right," the man said, exhaling. "I had a bag when you picked me up."

"So?"

"I'll need it."

LaPorta thought for a moment.

"Stay put."

He rose and, locking the door behind him, went to his office and retrieved a faded leather satchel. He returned and handed it to the man, who reached inside and pulled out a composition notebook with a black marble cover. On the label were nine handwritten words: *For the Boss, To Be Read Upon My Death.*

He pushed it across the table.

"What?" LaPorta said. "I should read this?"

"Only if you want answers."

The detective leafed through the handwritten pages.

"What is it?" he mumbled.

The man almost smiled.

"A love story," he said.

THE COMPOSITION BOOK

Dear Boss,

So how do I begin? That I'm dying? I suspect you know that by now. The other day you came into the beach house and found me on the floor by the laundry basket with my left leg splayed out and my head on my elbow and you said, "Alfie, what are you doing?" and I said, "I'm looking for ants." You smiled but I could see in your eyes a genuine concern, and as you helped me to my feet there was a gentleness in your touch, the way your arm hooked under mine, the way your fingers spread against my back. If I didn't know better, I might call it a loving embrace. But I do know better. It's knowing better that leads me to this confession.

I'm not afraid of dying, Boss. I know you tell me not to call you "Boss," but hey, you pay my salary, and I guess I'm old-fashioned. Anyhow, I'm not afraid. I've skirted death many times. That may sound exaggerated. It's not.

In my long life—and it's been far longer than anyone knows—I have leapt off a mountain in Spain, dived into a pool of sharks in Australia, stood in front of an oncoming train in China, even taken a bullet during a Mexican bank robbery.

I did most of these things to see what it was like, to feel the breath of God or the devil or whatever awaits me when this life is over. It wasn't courage. I knew I would survive.

The reason I knew will be difficult to believe, Boss, but please try, because I've been waiting a long time to tell you.

All right. Here goes.

I get to do things twice.

I mean it. I get a second chance at everything. Do-overs. Rollbacks. Whatever you want to call them. It's a gift. A power. There's no explanation. But while everyone in the world must suffer the consequences of their actions, I can undo mine and try again. Not endless chances, mind you. I can't keep messing up and wiping the slate clean. Can't take the same test a hundred times.

Twice. I get two shots at everything. The thing is, I have to live with my second try. There's no going back. Over the years, I have found this to be the price that I pay for this gift.

And the price I have paid in love.

I've had one great love in my life, Boss. One woman in whose eyes I found the better version of myself. But I made a grave mistake, one I could *not* go back and fix. It's a cruel trick to have two chances at your heart's desire. It can make—

NASSAU

LaPorta stopped reading and looked up from the notebook.

"You're screwing with me, right?"

"I'm sorry?"

"You want me to believe you can go back in time and correct things?"

"If I choose to, yes."

LaPorta chuckled. "I doubt that will hold up in court."

"It's the truth."

"Who's your boss?"

"Doesn't matter."

"It will if he helped plan your crimes."

"My boss is a woman. And she didn't."

LaPorta scratched his eyebrow.

"You're really dying?"

The man nodded.

"Of what?"

"Does it matter? Neurological."

"Sorry to hear." LaPorta sat back in his chair. "If I were dying, I sure as hell wouldn't be writing a farewell note to *my* boss, I can tell you that much."

"Keep reading."

"You really want this as your alibi?"

"You asked."

"Is it because of—what's her name—Gianna Rule?"

The man looked away.

"Well, then, by all means, let's keep going," LaPorta said. "But from now on . . ."

He slid the notebook across the table.

"*You* read it. Out loud."

Then he added, almost mockingly, "*Alfie.*"

THE COMPOSITION BOOK

OK, Boss. Assuming you haven't thrown this notebook away by now, dismissed it as the ramblings of a longtime employee/friend whose time has come and whose mind has gone a bit cuckoo, I will tell you how I learned of my unique power, and when I first discovered it, by accident, as a child.

It was 1966. A Saturday morning. I was eight years old, and we were living in Kenya, in a small village north of Mombasa. My parents were missionaries. New ones. In their mid-thirties they'd heard the call to spread the Lord's gospel. At least my mother did. My father went along dutifully, perhaps hoping the Holy Spirit would embrace him at the airport.

We'd been there for a year, living in a thatched roof cabin with a pull-chain toilet. Before Africa, we had lived just outside Philadelphia. I missed it terribly. I hated the relentless sun of this new continent. There was no television and little for me to do. My mother discovered an old piano in the village church, and she taught me just enough chords to play a few hymns. One Sunday she gathered the local kids in a circle and made me sing "Nearer My God to Thee." They laughed at my voice. I wanted to disappear.

I made two friends the whole time I was in Africa, one human, one animal. The animal was an elephant named Lallu. She belonged to a nearby rancher, who used her for pulling plows. On Saturdays, he let Lallu rest, and I got to play with her. She would coil her trunk around me and lift me up. It was scary at first, but over time, it felt strangely protective.

Lallu was responsible for my second friend, a wiry girl with piercing green eyes and dark hair cut in pageboy bangs. Her mother was from the Philippines, but her father was American. He had been transferred to Kenya with Del Monte foods, and on Saturdays he would bring his daughter to play with Lallu as well.

We'd take turns being lifted. But we were impatient. You know how kids are. One time, as we jockeyed for position, the elephant picked us both up together. I remember her small body squeezed next to mine, shoulder to shoulder. Our cheeks touched and we both hollered "Whoaaaa!" and when Lallu let us down, we started laughing so hard we couldn't stop.

That was the first time she told me her name. Princess. I said that's not a name. She said that's what everyone in her family called her. I said all right.

The next week, Princess brought me some red mabuyu sweets. The next week I brought her a sliced coconut. The next week she brought a book about butterflies and read it out loud under a tree. The next week, we held hands when Lallu scooped us up. From then on, we did it every time.

When you are lonely and you suddenly find a friend, it fills up your world. Although I was just eight years old, my time with Princess felt like something more than companionship. Puppy love, I guess. Saturdays became the only thing I looked forward to.

The last time I saw Princess, Lallu sprayed us both with water and we had to change clothes in the trees. I peeked at her naked back as she pulled a borrowed shirt over her head. She turned, caught me looking, and smiled.

"We should build a house here one day, Alfie, by the ocean. And then we can get married and Lallu can live with us. OK?"

"OK," I said.

She smiled. I smiled back. I felt the afternoon sun drying my skin. It's the best memory I have of Africa.

Then came the worst.

*

Eleven months into our stay, my mother got sick from a bug that bit her and had to go to the hospital, where she remained for several weeks. When she came home, she was thin and weak, but I took her return as a sign she was getting better.

I had been into comic books back in the States, and before we'd departed, I'd begged my father for a Superman costume. In Kenya, I slept every night with the red cape on. A reminder of home, I suppose.

When I awoke that particular Saturday morning, I bounced to the mirror with my red cape over my white undershirt and posed, hands on hips, flexing what little muscle I had.

"What are you doing?"

My father was at the door. I dropped my arms.

"Nothing."

"Go sit with your mother."

"Why?"

"Just go sit with your mother."

"Why?"

"Because I told you to, that's why."

"But I haven't had breakfast yet."

"Do as I say. I'm going to get her medicine."

"Can I go?"

"No."

"I'm still going to play with Lallu later, right?"

"We'll see. Go sit with your mother. Move it."

I dragged down the small hallway until I heard the front door shut. I peeked in my parents' room. My mother was in bed, her eyes closed under the white mosquito netting. I held there, listening to her breathe. I told myself if she didn't stir within a minute, I wasn't supposed to wake her, and I should go outside and play.

A minute passed. Absolving myself, I scooted out the door and ran to the local soccer field, which was really just a large patch of cinnamon-colored dirt. It was empty, so I raced from one end to the next, my cape flapping behind me, leaping every fifth step, as if I might lift into the air.

The sun was high and the breeze was light. After many failed launches, I lay down in some nearby kikuyu grass and stared up at the long white clouds. Eventually, I nodded off.

When I awoke, I meandered through the village. I caught the usual stares of our neighbors. The red cape didn't help. I passed the church where my parents worked and saw the local pastor, his tweed suit coat draping a clerical collar.

He was tending a goat. I waved. He waved back. The goat bleated. It was almost noon.

I walked back home in the oppressive heat, listening to my sneakers grind the gravelly dirt. I noticed a green jeep parked in front of our cabin. When I entered, I heard mumbled conversation, then my father yelling, "Alfie? Is that you? Alfie, don't come in here!"

Suddenly, he was in front of me, having shut the bedroom door behind him.

"Where did you go?"

His voice sounded wobbly.

"Mom was sleeping so I went out."

"You went out?" He bit his knuckles. "You went *out*?"

I remember him glaring, as if that were the cruelest thing I could have said. I didn't understand. What had I done? It was only when I saw a doctor exit the bedroom that I had the sense something terrible had just happened, and that, in playing Superman on a soccer field, I'd missed it.

*

My mother died while I was trying to fly. A pulmonary embolism. From what they told me, she went quickly and "didn't suffer," but since no one was there, I'm not sure how they knew. I remember sitting on my mattress that night, sobbing, gagging on my breath, then sobbing again. Down the hall, I heard my father turn up the radio, really loud, then make a terrible howling noise, like a bear with its paw caught in a trap.

Before I went to sleep, I threw my red cape out the bedroom window. I watched the wind blow it across the dirt. I returned to bed wishing the day had never happened, hating Africa, hating Superman, hating myself, and missing my mother in every molecule of hot air being moved around the room by a plastic fan. I slapped my body repeatedly, whispering the words "stupid, stupid." It began to storm outside and I fell asleep to the sound of rain.

*

When I awoke the next morning, the red cape was somehow draped around me again. My eyes were blurry. I heard my father's heavy feet enter the room.

"What are you doing?"

"Nothing."

"Go sit with your mother."

"What?"

"Go sit with your mother."

I swallowed.

"How?"

"What do you mean how? Go sit with her. I'm going to get her medicine."

I know this sounds impossible, Boss. I can only tell you that it happened, and that I went along with it, the way you go along with a dream, even to someplace you don't want to go. I reached my mother's room. The door was open. When I finally looked inside, she was sleeping under the netting, just like the day before.

Had I been older, I might have run off screaming. But as an eight-year-old boy, I just wanted to be with her, no matter how impossible it seemed. So I stood there, frozen, until my mother's eyes opened and she saw me hovering, and she smiled and hoarsely whispered, "Well, hello, Superman."

I must have recoiled, because it registered on her face.

"Alfie? What's wrong?"

I couldn't answer. My breath came in puffs.

"Alfie? Tell me."

"Mom . . . ?" I whispered.

"Oh, no." Her expression changed. "Alfie? Have you been here before?"

"Uh-huh."

"And the last time, did something bad happen?"

"Yes."

"Did I die?"

I nodded.

"And you saw that?"

"No . . . I . . . I went out to . . ."

I started crying.

"I'm sorry, Mommy."

She took a deep breath. Her voice rose. "We don't have much time, then, sweetheart. Listen to me." She pulled the netting aside, leaned forward, and put my face between her hands. "This is something you're going to be able to do the rest of your life. Get second chances. Do you understand?"

I shook my head no.

"It's a gift. A power. Some people in our family get it.

You're blessed to be one of them. But it won't fix everything, Alfie. The second time won't always be better than the first."

She squeezed my hand. "Don't try and change everything, OK? Don't correct every mistake. Don't take advantage of people. Don't use your power for money. Be careful. Do you hear me, Alfie? Alfie, are you listening?"

I felt like I was suffocating.

"Mom," I blurted out, "are you going to die again?"

She bit her lip, then patted a space on the edge of the bed.

"Sit here, baby," she said, forcing a smile. "Let me tell you all the things I love about you."

*

Now, in case you're wondering, Boss, my mother still died that morning, this time in front of me, after listing a dozen or so things she loved about her only child. I saw her grab her arm, I heard her groan, I watched her head roll back. My father returned and found me weeping against the bed, the mosquito netting hanging over my face.

This is when I first learned the limits of my "gift": I can't change mortality. If someone's time is up, it's up. I can travel back to before the death takes place. I can alter how I experience it. But it's still going to happen. Nothing I can do to stop it.

Can I say it was better, rewinding my mom's departure? I don't know. The first time, I left the house and returned motherless. The second time, I stood witness as she departed this world. You tell me.

NASSAU

Alfie looked up from the pages. LaPorta was staring.

"You've got some imagination. I'll give you that."

"I didn't imagine it," Alfie said.

"Sure, you didn't."

LaPorta rocked slowly in his chair.

"It's a weird name. 'Alfie.' You don't hear it very often."

"No."

"Your passport says Alfred."

"My father's father's name. My mother said it sounded like a British lord. She started calling me Alfie after that song."

"What song?"

"From the '60s. 'What's it all about, Alfie?'"

"Oh, right."

"If I had a dollar for every time someone sang that to me—"

"You'd have as much money as you stole?"

Alfie smiled. "I didn't steal anything."

"Really? You immediately wired your winnings to some woman, and we picked you up the next morning at a travel agency, buying tickets to Africa."

"So?"

"Sooo, that sounds a lot like a guy trying to run and hide from something."

"The tickets weren't for me."

"Who were they for?"

"If you just let me finish this—"

"Yeah, yeah. Your alibi notebook. I know."

LaPorta checked his phone. No message yet from the Bahamian police. He sighed. Things took forever in the islands.

"It's from a movie, isn't it?" LaPorta said. "That song? *Alfie*?"

"Yes. A movie about a playboy who gets all these women to fall in love with him, but eventually pays a price."

"So that's you? A playboy?"

"No. Just the guy who paid a price."

"Well, I don't give a crap. How's that? When do we get to the roulette scheme?"

"I told you. It's part of the story."

LaPorta drummed his fingernails on the table.

"Come on then, playboy. Keep reading."

THE COMPOSITION BOOK

My father and I moved back to America, to our old neighborhood outside Philadelphia. My mother was buried a few miles away, in a cemetery just off the highway. I remember the constant whoosh of traffic as they lowered her casket into the ground. It felt so disrespectful, people driving past, going to work, listening to their radios. I put my hands over my ears. I didn't hear most of what the pastor said.

After everyone left, I stood there with my father, staring at the grave.

"Why do they throw dirt in there?" I asked.

"That's just how they do it, Alfie."

"Mom didn't like dirt."

"No, she didn't."

"Dad?"

"Yeah?"

"Should we clean it out?"

He bit his lip and squeezed my shoulder. The wind blew. I think that was the moment I realized it was just him and me now.

*

We settled into a small Colonial-style house and I started wearing long sleeves again. I watched television. I snacked on Scooter Pies. Everything from Africa felt like a dream. Someone in our church offered my father the old Baldwin piano my mother used to play, and he put it in the basement. I spent a lot of time down there, trying to remember the hymns she had taught me.

It took some time before I repeated my "magic." My mother's second death was an unsettling memory, and I was in no hurry to go through something like that again. I hadn't told anyone, not even my dad. Part of me wasn't sure it ever really happened.

Then, a few months after we'd returned from Africa, I experienced it again. I was on my way home from school, me and my walking buddies from the neighborhood, Stewie, Sandy, and Paul. It was a gray afternoon, and a cold rain was falling. We passed a small, rickety A-frame home with faded brown shutters and a muddy swath of dead leaves covering the grass.

"Witch's house," Sandy mumbled.

We called it that because every now and then kids in the neighborhood would spot a crouched, white-haired woman staring out through the flimsy screen door. The legend was that one Halloween she had pulled a trick-or-treater inside, and when he came out, he was never the same. I have no idea if the story is true. We were just kids.

Suddenly, Stewie blurted out: "Yo, Alfie, I dare you to knock on her door."

The others joined in.

"Yeah, Alfie!" "Do it!" "Don't be scared, Alfie!" "C'mon!"

I looked away. My mother's death had dealt a huge blow to my confidence. I found it hard to engage with people, especially neighbors who whispered, "They never should have gone to Africa." I missed my mother terribly, the long, meandering conversations we had over peanut butter crackers in our kitchen, and the way she rubbed my hair after kissing me good night.

Without her, our house was unbearably silent. At night, my father would stare at the black-and-white TV. I would lie on the couch and cover my eyes with the back of my hands. Sometimes my heart would begin to race and I found it hard to breathe. I coughed and choked. My father would ask, "What's wrong, Alfie?" But I didn't know myself. I just wanted to stop feeling scared all the time, worrying that another bad thing was going to happen.

That day at the witch's house, it seemed to come to a head. I was tired of being frightened and I didn't want the boys calling me chicken all the way home. So I accepted their challenge and moved slowly toward the door. I stopped a short distance from the screen, not wanting to be snatched if the witch suddenly appeared.

"Hurry up, before she sees you!" Stewie whisper-yelled.

"Or kills you," Sandy added.

They laughed. I quickly lost my nerve. *Why had I agreed to this?* I leaned forward at the waist. My entire body was trembling. I stretched toward the door, squeezed my eyes shut, and made my fist knock. Once.

Then I ran away.

I ran as fast as I can ever remember running, my feet making wide leaps over the street puddles. Tears were streaming down my cheeks. In my mind I saw my mother's face, lying on her deathbed, looking at me as if I were pathetic. In the distance, I heard the cackling laughter of my three friends, and Stewie shouting, "There's no one home, stupid!" By then it was too late. I had shown my true colors, and they were the yellows of cowardice.

I couldn't sleep that night. I dreaded having to face those boys again. I so wanted to erase what happened at the witch's house that for the first time, I considered what my mother had told me. (*This is something you're going to be able to do the rest of your life. Get second chances.*) If that were true, I was ready to try.

I replicated what I'd done on the night my mother died. I wished the day had never happened. I tapped my thighs. I even mumbled the words "stupid, stupid," in case I needed to repeat everything exactly.

The next morning, when I awoke, the cold, drizzly weather was the same as the day before, and when we walked to school, the boys were wearing the same clothes and none of them said anything about the incident. In class, we covered the same pages in the history book. We took the same spelling test.

I was stunned. Everything was repeating itself. I moved through the day in blinking wonderment, knowing exactly what was going to happen and watching it unfold.

Even the walk home went as it had previously gone, right up to the moment when Sandy mumbled, "Witch's house."

Which is when I changed the story.

"Let's see if she's in there," I blurted out.

The others gaped at me.

"What's the matter?" I said. "Are you scared?"

"No way," Paul said.

"Nuh-uh," Sandy said.

"I dare you," Stewie said, crossing his arms.

I glared at him, anger and excitement mixing in my gut.

"Watch me," I said.

Watch me? I had never uttered those words before. I was the kind of kid who didn't want other people looking at him. *Watch me?* I walked steadily to the front door.

"Still dare me?" I said, looking back.

"You won't do it," Stewie insisted.

I took a deep breath, planted my feet, and banged. Then I banged again. Knowing she wasn't home, I shot a glance at my disbelieving friends, then screamed, "Come out, Witch! Show your ugly face!"

That did it. Sandy, Stewie, and Paul bolted down the street, just as I had the day before. As I watched them run, I was flushed with a new sensation, one that would shape my life going forward. Knowing what's going to happen before it happens is more than a unique power. It's godlike.

And that is how I felt.

*

Now, at this point, Boss, you probably have questions, the kind that always come with time travel stories. What happens if you step on a butterfly, that sort of thing? Let me clear things up right here. I'm not a comic book hero. I can't wave my hand and go frolicking with dinosaurs or zap myself onto the deck of the *Titanic*.

Unless it happened to me, I have no way of revisiting it. I can select any moment in my own life and change it once. But after it's changed, I'm stuck with that new version going forward.

I'm more of a duplicator, really, a reshaper of my own existence. If you interacted with me, then I can change that experience, and you'll have no recollection of our previous encounter.

But I will.

That's the price I pay.

NASSAU

LaPorta laughed out loud.

"What?" Alfie said, glancing up from the notebook.

"For a guy who stole a couple million bucks, you sure feel sorry for yourself."

"You think this is a joke?"

LaPorta nodded sarcastically. "Yes. I. do."

"Can I ask you a question, then?"

"I can't wait."

"Why do you think I wrote all this down?"

"I don't know, Alfred 'Alfie' Logan. Because you're crazy? Because criminals often exhibit weird behavior?"

"And if I told you this notebook will prove I'm not a criminal?"

"I thought you said it was a love story. You should make up your mind."

LaPorta glanced at his watch. It was almost noon. He popped another Life Saver into his mouth.

"Giving up smoking?" Alfie asked.

"How'd you know? Wait. Don't tell me. You traveled back in time and saw me light up."

Alfie sighed. "You're not taking me seriously."

LaPorta rolled the candy slowly over his tongue. He *did* wish it were a cigarette.

"Keep reading," he said.

THE COMPOSITION BOOK

I'll move the story along now, Boss, because there is much to share and I don't want to lose the point, which is to tell you of the one great love in my life, and what I'd like you to do for her after I'm gone.

For the rest of my childhood, my father and I remained in that same Colonial home with our Plymouth Road Runner in the driveway. We rarely went anywhere. My parents used to go shopping, eat at restaurants, play gin rummy with the neighbors. But my mother's death had left my dad rudderless. He worked. He came home. Now and then, when the weather was warm, he'd toss a baseball with me, but he always seemed distracted, his thoughts elsewhere.

We never spoke about Africa. But there was a photo of my mom on the table next to the couch, and I often caught my father studying it, as if he couldn't turn away, the way someone stares at a bad medical report. We'd stopped going to church. We no longer prayed before meals. I think Dad felt if this was how God treated those who went around the world to spread His Good News, he'd just as soon sit things out.

Looking back, I felt badly for him. It must have been hard, living alone with me, because in those days a single man with a child was pretty rare. He wasn't exactly welcome around other married couples, but he was too old to be hanging out with the local single men, most of whom were just a few years out of high school. He largely let me do what I wanted and tolerated my banging on the basement piano. He even bought me a cheap Radio Shack microphone for singing.

But he did make one thing abundantly clear: rules. No leaving the kitchen before the dishes were washed. No exiting the bathroom unless the dirty towels were in the hamper. No television during the day. No loud music at night.

In the silent vacuum of my mother's absence, rules were what my father used to reset his balance.

I had my own resets.

*

My mother had been right. I *was* able to do anything twice. It took me a while to master the technique, like a baby Superman learning to fly. But once I got the hang of it, I began taking second chances at anything that went wrong the first go-around. What kid wouldn't? A bad grade on a spelling test? I went back and aced it. A strikeout in a baseball game? I relived the at bat, this time knowing what pitches to expect. If I mouthed off and got punished, I repeated the encounter and kept my mouth shut the second time. Consequently, I rarely paid a price for bad behavior. And unlike most kids, I was never bruised or bloodied for more than a few seconds. As long as I could jump back in time, I could unbreak every broken bone and untwist every twisted ankle. Physical danger became a challenge. When other boys my age thought risk-taking meant looking up *fart* in the dictionary, I was skating into holes on the ice or jumping off the roof over our garage.

Best of all, this power enabled me to undo the embarrassments of my often-distracted personality. Once, in fourth grade, I was staring out the window, daydreaming, when the teacher asked me to "name any one of the classification of organisms."

I froze.

"Organisms?" I said.

"Yes, Alfie. Name one."

All I could think of was the "organ" part.

"The kind you play in church?"

The room erupted in laughter. Tommy Helms, who was nearly twice my size and a brute on the football field, blurted out, "He's an idiot. He doesn't even have a mother." The teacher turned to scold him, but before she finished her sentence, I had transported myself back to the breakfast table that morning, where, over a bowl of Cocoa Puffs, I opened my science book and began memorizing.

Later that day, while I was staring out the window—deliberately this time—the teacher asked me the same question, and I turned to her slowly.

"Organisms?"

"Yes, Alfie. Name one."

I saw Tommy Helms sneering. I waited for maximum effect. Then I stood up.

"Domain, kingdom, phylum, class, order, family, genus, and species."

My teacher blinked. "Yes. Wow. That's all of them. Excellent, Alfie."

I gave Tommy a look, then sat back down. It was all I could do to keep from laughing.

*

You may have noticed I no longer had to sleep to make my second chances happen. Nor did I have to call myself "stupid." Through trial and error, I learned I only had to say or think the word *twice* and tap any part of my body. That took me back to somewhere earlier that day. If I wanted to go back further, I could, but I had to focus on the event I wanted to revisit.

This required meticulous record-keeping. I began to chart my daily activities in composition notebooks. When I got up. Where I rode my bike. Who I ate lunch with at school.

"Why are you always writing in those notebooks?" my dad asked.

"I like to keep track of things."

"Like a diary?"

"No. Diaries are for girls."

The truth was, I needed data to make my jumps. Otherwise, I might repeat something unintended, which sometimes happened anyway.

One day I was craving chocolate ice cream really badly, so I focused on my last visit to Custard King, which I remembered as two weeks earlier with my father. I pictured the car ride in my head. I mumbled *twice*, tapped my leg, and instantly landed in the backseat of our Plymouth. Only then did I see empty cups and discarded spoons on the floor, and I realized I had remembered it incorrectly. I had actually walked to Custard King with friends, and Dad had picked us up. So not only was there no ice cream that day, but I was stuck reliving the next two weeks all over again.

And yes, I have to go forward in real time. No skipping back to the present. I return to the age I was with each jump and continue on from there.

Which is why I say that nobody knows how long I have been on this earth. If you took all the repeated hours, days, months, and years, I would guess it is many lifetimes. It feels that way, anyhow.

*

My best friend during those years was a kid named Wesley, who was older than me but for some reason didn't start school until he was seven, so we were in the same grade. We didn't have a lot of Black families in our neighborhood, and he and his younger sister, London, were constantly getting picked on. Maybe that's why we took to each other. That, and I had been to Africa, which his parents seemed to like.

Wesley wore horn-rimmed glasses and built model rocket ships in his basement. When America sent Apollo 11 to the moon, he was so excited, he kept a daily scrapbook. He cut up newspaper stories and pasted them on dated pages labeled with colorful penmanship. It was meticulous, and he was rightly proud of it. One day, for science class, he brought that scrapbook to school.

As we walked down the hallway, a couple of older boys surrounded us and demanded to see what Wesley was holding. One of them was Alan Ponto, a loud, stocky kid who was already growing whiskers on his chin. He leafed through the scrapbook and said, "Hey, this page is cool."

"Thanks," Wesley said.

"Wanna know what makes it cooler?"

He tore the page out, ripped it in half, then ripped up the pieces. "That's cooler."

Wesley burst into tears.

"Aw, did I make the little nerd cry?" Alan mocked.

Poor Wesley. Crying was the worst thing he could have done. A group of students quickly gathered, laughing as he wiped his eyes and hugged his scrapbook to his chest.

I felt so bad for him that I tapped back to when Wesley and I were walking to school. I thought about telling him to hide his scrapbook in his desk. Then I decided on something else. Once inside, I ran to the science teacher, Mr. Timmons, and told him to come quickly, some boys were threatening to destroy Wesley's project. We arrived just as Alan was tearing the page out.

"Young man, what are you doing?" Mr. Timmons said.

Alan spun around, surprised.

"Huh?"

"You just desecrated another student's work. Do you think that's funny?"

"Huh?"

The kids who had previously gathered to mock Wesley

were now poking each other. Many had been victims of Alan's bullying; they weren't missing his comeuppance.

"Can you tell me the properties of tape, Alan?"

"Huh?"

"The properties of tape," Mr. Timmons said. "Polypropylene, for starters. You're going to learn a lot about them, since you'll be taping every bit of that page very carefully back into Wesley's scrapbook."

"Huh?"

"Young man, do you know any words besides *Huh*?"

At that point, even Wesley cracked a smile.

He taught me something that morning. He taught me that this gift I have could actually make things better for *other* people. You might think, having learned this, that I spent the rest of my life in altruistic endeavors.

I didn't. I wish I had. The truth is, you never do as much good as you could.

*

Things my mother said she loved about me:

1. *"Your laugh."*
2. *"How you sleep with your arms under your pillow."*
3. *"Your courage, even when you're scared."*

One day, during a field trip to the zoo with my sixth-grade class, I was standing with a couple of girls near the lion exhibit. One of the girls was named Esther, and I kind of liked her, in the way that a sixth-grade boy likes a girl, which is awkward and without reciprocation. I was stealing a glance at her pinkish cheeks when one of the big cats roared, and I jumped backward.

"You got spooked," Esther said, giggling.

"No, I didn't."

"Yes, you did! I thought you lived in Africa. Aren't you used to lions?"

I looked away. My new response to embarrassment like this was a quick time jump to correct it. But hoping to impress Esther, I took a bolder tact.

"Lions don't scare me," I bragged. "If I wanted to, I could play with them right now."

"Play with lions?"

"Sure. We did it every day in Africa."

(We did no such thing. I saw one lion the entire time I was there.)

Quickly, Esther's friends jumped in. "Do it!" "I dare you!" "I double dare you!" But Esther changed her tone. "Wait, you're messing around, right, Alfie?"

I straightened up, chuff with phony bravery.

"Watch me."

The exhibit was protected by a high fence, then a long space, then a wall behind which the lions roamed freely. Reminding myself all I had to do was tap my body and say *twice*, I jumped onto the fence and shimmied up. I heard Esther yell, "Alfie, no!" but I was already over. I looked back and grinned at the girls with their hands over their mouths.

I saw two lions lift their heads and one rise on its paws. I trembled but kept moving forward. I could hear the screams of people beyond the fence. Another step. Another step. The largest lion began pacing, eyeballing me. Although I had done this to impress a girl, I was now hypnotized by the danger. I eased over the low stone wall and took two more strides in the animals' direction.

The lion growled. I saw his ears flatten and his tail sweep from side to side. Then, just like that, he broke into a sprint, charging straight at me, head low, mouth open. I slapped my legs, yelled "*Twice!*" and immediately was face down in my pillow that morning, my heart going like a drill.

I lay there for a minute, the sunlight spilling through the window, still seeing that beast coming at me. It was frightening, yes. But exhilarating. As alive as I've ever felt. I could have died in that moment, Boss, yet I didn't. And I foolishly gave myself the credit for that. It was the start of an addiction to invincibility. A belief that nothing I did the first time could hurt me.

It was also a realization that, for all these chances I was taking, I was the only one to reflect on my bravery. Later that day, when our class (again) went to the zoo, I stood next to Esther. When that lion roared, I didn't flinch. I didn't say a thing. I wanted to brag, "Hey, I just ran into his cage! He was this close to eating me!" But it's not like I had any proof. My first chances let me be Superman. My second chances, I was stuck as Clark Kent.

NASSAU

"Wait," LaPorta said. "What year was that? The lion cage thing?"

"I'm not sure," Alfie said. "Maybe 1969, or '70?"

"An incident like that would be reported. Even written about in a local newspaper."

"Probably."

"I can cross-check it in a database. We can prove if your story is true right now. Where did you say that happened? Philadelphia?"

He rose from his seat.

"You're wasting your time, Detective."

LaPorta turned. "Why?"

"Once I undo something, no record of my first actions exists. That was one reality, but we're in this one now. The one where I just stood there and never approached that cage."

"What are you talking about?" LaPorta snapped.

"I can't explain the physics. I can only tell you that my second-chance life is the one the rest of this world is witnessing. I'm the only one who remembers the things I undid."

"And that means . . . ?"

"It means you're not going to find anything."

LaPorta rubbed his chin. He held for a moment. Then he dropped back into his chair.

"Well, isn't that convenient for you."

He took out his phone and pressed a number.

"Who are you calling?" Alfie asked.

"I ask the questions," LaPorta replied.

Actually, he was still trying to reach his contact with the Bahamian police, a young officer named Sampson, who was supposed to be rounding up the casino staff for questioning. When no one answered, he hung up the phone and blew out a mouthful of air.

"Shall I continue?" Alfie asked.

"For now," LaPorta said.

Two

THE COMPOSITION BOOK

Since I mentioned Esther, Boss, I should get to how this power affected me in love. I find myself clinging to that subject these days. Who I've loved. Who's loved me back. Who will keep me company in my final days? When we're young, we want to satisfy every desire. When we're old, our greatest desire is to not die alone.

Love began to interest me when I was twelve. Up to that point, I'd been awkward around girls. And, as a short, skinny kid, I worried I always would be. To be honest, the only time I'd felt comfortable with a girl was back in Africa, when Princess and I were being scooped up together in an elephant's trunk. I sometimes wondered where she was now.

Then adolescence arrived. Girls began developing. Boys began noticing. Hormones raged, and by junior high, kids were having what we called "make-out parties." They all had the same ingredients: a basement, a record player, a black light, and most importantly, parents who were gone for the evening. I made the mistake of mentioning these parties to my father once, who responded with, "I better not catch you at one of those, or it'll be the last party you ever attend."

Of course, that only made me want to go more. One Saturday, my friend Stewie, who was now a full head taller than me, mentioned a get-together at a girl's house in the neighborhood. Her name was Robin. She lived on a cul-de-sac.

"There's gonna be making out," he said. "We should go."

"Can Wesley come?" I asked.

"I'm asking you, not him. We don't want too many boys there!"

I stayed home at first, partly out of loyalty to Wesley, but also out of fear. I'd never even kissed a girl. I didn't think I could fake my way through it. But then my father went out, and the house grew so quiet that curiosity got the best of me. I could always tap out if things got too weird, right?

I quickly showered and dressed in my newest jeans and a tie-dyed T-shirt. Thinking about the girls who would be there, I spritzed some of my father's aftershave on my neck and cheeks. I left the back door unlocked so I could sneak in later.

The "party" consisted of nine kids: four girls, five boys. After sitting around listening to music for a while, Robin suggested we play a game called Seven Minutes in Heaven, where couples went into a closet and stayed there for seven minutes.

"We have to pair up," Robin said, smiling at Stewie, who smiled back. Robin was one of the popular kids in our class. She wore dark bangs over her forehead and silver gloss on her lips. "Also," she said, "one of you boys will have to sit out, because there's not enough girls to match up."

"I'll sit," I quickly offered.

"No, not you." She pointed to Herman, a sixth grader with a crew cut who had only been invited because he was another girl's brother. "You."

Herman looked relieved. The rest of us paired off. I was matched with a skinny girl named Adrian, who had braces on her teeth and wore wide bell-bottom jeans. We sat next to each other as Stewie and Robin went into the closet first, while a kid named Pete checked his watch. When seven minutes passed, Pete banged on the door and the closet opened. Robin emerged, her shirt untucked. She was fanning herself.

"I want more time!" she squealed. Stewie grinned. The rest of us laughed nervously. These two had clearly moved up the coolness scale.

Next, it was our turn. Adrian rose and walked to the closet. I followed behind, my heart thumping so hard I swore the others could hear it.

"Don't do anything I wouldn't do," Stewie cracked.

To say those next seven minutes were excruciating would be underselling it. I barely knew Adrian. I could only see her silhouette. For a while, we said nothing.

"Do you think they really made out?" she finally whispered.

"Who, Stewie and Robin?" I whispered back.

"Yeah."

"I don't know. What do you think?"

"I don't know."

"Me neither."

Silence.

"Do you think she likes him?" I asked.

"I heard she did."

"Yeah?"

"She told Alison. She wrote him a note."

"What did it say?"

"I don't know. I just heard she did it."

"Oh."

It went on like this, with muffled music coming from under the door. Our eyes adjusted and Adrian's shape became more visible in the darkness, as did the shelves and boxes in the closet. I felt like I needed to advance things in some way, so I edged closer and nervously slid my hand onto her arm. I moved it down until my palm rested on the top of her fingers. She wiggled them uncomfortably.

"You smell funny," she said.

"I do?"

"Like my dad."

The aftershave. I swallowed hard. After that, I couldn't think of a single thing to say.

"We don't have to make out," she finally offered.

"OK," I mumbled.

The rest of the time, we just sat in the darkness. A single minute never felt so long. When we finally emerged—to a chorus of "whoo-hoos"—I noticed Adrian shoot Robin a look and shake her head no. Stewie saw this, too.

"They didn't do anything!" he yelled. "I knew it!" He pointed at me. "Wimp!"

As you probably guessed, I tapped out seconds later. I redid the whole event. This time I skipped the aftershave. And I walked to the party determined not to be so meek. When Robin suggested Seven Minutes in Heaven, I shouted,

"Cool! I love that game!" And once in the closet, I told Adrian, "You don't have to like me or anything, but I think we should kiss so that they don't make fun of us when we get out, OK?"

She seemed taken aback by my honesty.

"All right," she answered.

I edged closer, but since this was before our eyes adjusted, I banged my forehead into her ear, then my nose into hers.

"Ow," she said.

"Ow" is not a good prelude to a kiss, especially your first, but that's what it was for me. I pushed my face forward until my mouth found the area beneath her nostrils. I pressed on it the way a kid presses his lips on a frosted window. She pressed back, keeping her mouth tightly closed to avoid me feeling her braces. We did this twice. It was dry and unmemorable. Then we separated and spent the rest of the seven minutes whispering small talk. When we exited, I guess it looked as if we had done something, because all Stewie yelled out was, "Next!"

An hour later, I went home. I tiptoed through the back door to find my father waiting for me, his arms crossed. He grounded me for a month. I trudged upstairs, feeling numb.

Later, as I lay in bed staring out the window, I decided that making out was definitely not worth it. I was too young to understand the real reason for my gloom—that my first kiss had only come on a second try. Years later, I would wish I had saved that moment for someone else.

NASSAU

"Wait, let me guess," LaPorta said. "Gianna Rule. She's the 'someone else' you're talking about?"

"That's right."

"When do we get to her part?"

"Soon."

LaPorta rocked his chair up on its rear legs. "Listen, pal. I know where all this is going. You're going to tell me you used your little 'power' to travel back before each spin of the roulette wheel and play the winning number."

"Not exactly," Alfie said.

"Not exactly, huh? You think you're pretty smart."

"Actually, my story is one of great foolishness."

LaPorta dropped his chair down with a bang.

"Cut the crap, Shakespeare. You think I haven't noticed that, in your little fantasy here, you haven't once mentioned money? If I actually believed you could do what you're saying—which I don't—that's the first thing anyone would have done."

"My mother warned me against that, remember?"

"You could have bought a lottery ticket."

"I was too young."

"Go to the racetrack."

"I was just a kid. How would I go to a racetrack?"

LaPorta smirked. "We obviously didn't grow up in the same neighborhood."

He dug out another Life Saver and popped it into his mouth. He looked at his phone. Still no message.

"For me," he said, leaning back, "it was Spin the Bottle."

"What was?"

"My first kiss. A bunch of us, maybe ten or eleven years old, sitting in a circle. I got lucky. I spun and landed on Nancy Killington, the best-looking girl in the fifth grade. Planted a huge smooch on her."

He cocked his head. "It's more fun to kiss someone when they're good-looking, right?"

Alfie thought for a moment.

"Not always," he said.

THE COMPOSITION BOOK

I was a late bloomer when it came to adolescence, Boss. I didn't cross the five-foot mark until junior high. That summer I grew two inches, and during eighth grade I grew another three. My bones hurt. My calves and knees ached every night. But in the mirror, I noticed the new heights from which I was looking at myself. This part, I didn't want to redo. I spent my entire freshman year of high school almost never tapping out, because I didn't want to be shorter. For a while, I even stopped recording events in my notebooks, because I wasn't planning to repeat any of them.

By tenth grade, I had sprouted to over six feet. I was hungry all the time, but nothing I ate seemed to stick to me. I was a knobby assemblage of limbs and angles. I walked like a skeleton shuffling.

"Put on a belt," my father would scold me, "your pants keep falling down."

By the time I turned fifteen, girls had completely taken over my orbit. I found my eyes darting at them when we passed in the halls. I spent a stupid amount of time in front of the school bathroom mirrors, adjusting the way my thick hair fell over my ears and forehead, or wetting the cowlicks to keep them from sticking up. Although I'd heard a few girls say I was "cute," I hated the way I looked; my ears were too prominent, my brows too thick. I had a full mouth, which I hated. I wanted a flat upper lip because mustaches looked better over those, and I dreamed of growing a mustache and looking older.

I did a hundred push-ups every night to try and make my scrawny chest thicker. I rolled up the sleeves of my shirts, because I thought it made my shoulders look broader. I had gotten pretty good at music—my piano playing had led to guitar and bass playing as well—and I tried walking around with the aloof sneer of my favorite rock stars. But every time I caught my reflection, I looked like a fish.

Conversing with the opposite sex was also a challenge. Without a mother to advise me, I was lost.

"How do you know if a girl likes you?" I asked my father once.

"Hard to say, Alfie."

"Isn't there some clue?"

"Well, if she doesn't walk away when you say hello, you have a chance."

That wasn't much help. Although I had the power to erase bad first impressions, I still seemed vulnerable to every mistake. Once, at a local diner, a group of girls was sitting in a booth. I had a serious crush on one of them, Natalie, a sophomore who pinned her blond hair back with two pink clips. She seemed shy and friendly and sometimes smiled when I walked past her in school. My buddies and I were in another booth, and they egged me on to speak with her. One bet a dollar I couldn't hold Natalie's interest for a minute.

I slowly approached the table. I had a nervous habit of moving my hands when I spoke, and when I finally made eye contact with Natalie, I began to say, "Hi, how are y—" when my right wrist flicked forward and knocked a glass of chocolate milk into her lap.

Her elbows shot out sideways. "Oh my God!" she yelled. When she glared up from her now-soaked jeans, all I could mumble was: "Look at that."

Look at that?

Needless to say, I *twiced* myself out of that situation. But the second time didn't go much better. I avoided the chocolate milk but was so focused on controlling my hands, I ran out of things to say after hello. Once she rolled her eyes at her friends, I knew I was toast. I dug my palms into my pockets and walked straight to the men's room, where I hid for the next fifteen minutes. That was the end of my crush on Natalie. And the dollar.

*

It was about this time when my father, who had grown sideburns and let his hair lengthen beyond the crew-cut stage, came home with a bag of McDonald's cheeseburgers. He put two on a plate, slid it in front of me, and sat down across the table. As I unwrapped the yellow paper and took my first bite, he announced he was getting married.

"*What?*" I said, choking. "To who?"

"Her name is Adeline."

"Who is she?"

"She works as a Realtor."

"I don't understand. When did you meet her? When do

you see her? Why do you want to marry her?" All those questions belied the loudest one screaming in my brain: *What about Mom?*

"I know this is probably hard for you, Alfie. But it's time for me to have someone in my life."

"You have me," I mumbled.

He smiled. "Not a son. A wife. It's good for a man to have a wife. Adeline is a lovely woman. You'll see."

"How long have you known her?"

"Six months. We met at the bowling alley."

"Where is she going to live?"

"What do you mean? She's going to live here."

"With us?"

"Of course, with us."

I pictured this strange woman sharing his bed. Sharing his bathroom. Eating from our plates. I put down the cheeseburger and sat there tearing up, feeling like a wrecking ball had just knocked me clear out of my life.

"Dad?" I finally said.

"Yeah?"

"Is she going to take down the pictures of Mom?"

"Of course, not, Alfie. She's not like that."

But she was. Adeline and my father got married at a courthouse with three witnesses—her older sister, my dad's friend Larry, and me. An hour later, my new stepmother pulled her 1972 Chevy Impala into our driveway. She adjusted her big sunglasses as my father lugged in three orange Samsonite bags. It was mid-March, and there was still snow on our porch.

"I'm looking forward to getting to know you, Alfred," she said.

"Everyone calls me Alfie."

"But your given name is Alfred, right? That's what your father told me."

I felt a burn of betrayal. My father was giving up family secrets before the woman even ruffled a couch pillow.

"Anyhow, Alfie is a name for a little boy," she said. "You're hardly a little boy anymore. You're almost six feet tall."

"Six foot and a half inch."

She blinked, as if not used to being corrected.

"Six foot and a half inch then," she repeated. "Alfred."

We ate our first meal together that night in the kitchen. She made salmon croquettes, which I hated. The next day she packed me a lunch for school, tuna salad, which I also hated. That weekend my father insisted we all go for a drive, and she told him three times in less than an hour, "Slow down, Lawrence, you're going to cause an accident."

The following week, while I was down in the basement playing piano, the door opened and I heard her yell, "That's enough banging now, Alfred. It's after eight!"

Four months later, I came home to find new furniture in our living room. An egg-shaped chair, an alabaster couch with lime stripes, and a matching ottoman. Missing was our old end table, the one that held my mother's framed photograph.

And the photograph itself.

"Where's her picture?" I yelled.

"What picture?"

"My mother's!"

"Oh. It's in the closet for now, with some other things. We'll find a new place for it."

"Which closet?"

"Does it matter?"

"Tell me which closet!"

"In the hallway." She tried to change the subject. "How do you like our new furniture, Alfred? You haven't said anything."

"It's ugly."

Her neck actually moved backward an inch. "That was rude."

"Well, it's true. It's ugly as sin."

"Take that back. Take it back right now!"

"Fine," I groused. "I take it back."

I spent the next few hours in my bedroom, holding my mother's photo. Everything I feared was coming to pass. I had finally gotten used to life alone with my father. Now came this second family upheaval. I thought about that final conversation with my mom, when she patted the bed and said, "Let me tell you all the things I love about you." Somehow, I could never picture Adeline saying something like that.

So I made a decision. That night, during dinner, I expressed a sudden interest in how my dad and my new stepmother had met. My father mostly shrugged, saying, "Why does it matter?" But Adeline happily recounted the story: how she'd gone to a bowling alley on a date, but the man never showed due to car trouble. My dad, there with his league team, had gone to the bar for drinks and, noticing her alone, offered her a beer.

"One thing led to another," she said, rubbing the back of his neck, "and here we are."

I wanted to vomit.

But I pressed on until I learned the exact date of their meeting. Then I raced to my room and scurried through my notebooks. I read what I was doing earlier that day. It was a Wednesday. Typical routine. Breakfast. School. Lunch in the cafeteria. Things I could not specifically recall. But that afternoon, the notebook said, I'd gone skateboarding with Wesley at a local park. I remembered that. I closed my eyes and whispered *twice*.

Instantly, I was back at that park, steering my board up a ramp, then cruising back down. My body felt different. Smaller. Less solid. I didn't realize how much I'd grown in ten months.

"What time is it?" I yelled to Wesley.

"Four forty-five!" he yelled back. "Why?"

My father's bowling league started at six thirty. I had to think fast. I looked around for something dangerous. There was a small footbridge that covered a creek, with a three-foot ledge on each side.

I took a deep inhale, then revved my wheels and steered onto that ledge. Halfway along, I leapt into the air. I had zero confidence I could land back on my board—and I didn't. My foot hit the ledge, then my shin, then my knee and elbow. I flipped into the creek.

"Alfie!" Wesley yelled.

I needed stitches in three places, which was more damage than I'd intended to inflict. It was the first time I'd truly injured myself and allowed the suffering to continue. I was surprised at how much it hurt. But, as I'd hoped, my father was called, and he stayed with me at the emergency room. It took a while because the hospital was busy.

When we finally left, he touched my shoulder.

"You all right, Alfie?"

"I'm OK, Dad."

"I don't understand something. Wesley said you jumped off your skateboard?"

"Yeah."

"Why?"

"I don't know. It was stupid." I rubbed my sore knee as I stole a glance at his watch. It was after seven. "Dad? Can we eat at the diner tonight? I'm starving."

"Yeah, all right." He looked at me as if my very existence puzzled him. "What were you *thinking*, Alfie?"

"I guess I wasn't," I said.

But, of course, I was. Having tended to his son's emergency, my father never went bowling. He never met Adeline. He remained single.

And a certain photo remained on our end table.

Perhaps this sounds cruel, denying my father a second marriage. If it makes a difference, he found another partner four years later, a lovely woman named Monica, and they enjoyed each other's company for decades.

Can I say I regret what happened with Adeline? Honestly, I can't. A boy may not do everything for his mother. But he'll do anything for her memory.

*

Things my mother said she loved about me:

4. "The way you don't give up until you've figured it out."

One afternoon during my junior year, I was sitting by a baseball field with Wesley. He had developed into a great athlete, slim and tightly muscled, and I think a lot of girls secretly liked him. He was more confident socially than I was. Despite experiencing many crushes, I was yet to know any affection in return. No girl had ever written me a love note or dreamily scribbled my name on her three-ring binder.

"Can I ask you something, Wes?"

"Yeah?"

"If you liked a girl, and you had two chances to get her to like you back, what would you do differently the second time?"

Wesley thought for a moment. He was never afraid to take time to answer a question, a quality I found rare.

"Well," he said, digging a cleat into the dirt, "I guess I would use the first time to find out everything she liked and everything she didn't. And the second time I would just do all the stuff she liked."

Brilliant Wesley. I had always been so focused on correcting mistakes, I never thought of my first pass as a research opportunity. Armed with this new approach, I immediately set my sights on the loftiest target: our classmate Jo Ann Donnigan, who could sing like a professional and got all the leads in the school plays. She had straight auburn hair, a delicately upturned nose, and had already won several local beauty pageants. She never arrived at school without looking as if she could go directly to a fancy restaurant. I'd had a secret crush on her since freshman year, but on the scales of high school popularity, she was way out of my league.

That was the challenge. We'd never spoken a word. But I did sit across from her in homeroom. The morning after my conversation with Wesley, I noticed her notebook had the cover of David Bowie's *Diamond Dogs* album on it. I summoned all my courage and, remembering this was just the first go-around, leaned in toward her.

"Hey, Jo Ann, do you like David Bowie?"

She scowled, as if wondering what gave me the right to speak to her.

"David Bowie?" I repeated. "You like him?"

She rolled her eyes.

"Everyone calls him Bowie," she said flatly.

"Yeah. Right. Bowie. So . . . what do you like about him?"

She sighed. "I dunno. How he dresses. His hair."

"Yeah."

"And his makeup. Even though he's a guy."

I shrugged. "If I came home in makeup, my father would shoot me."

She snorted, which I took as a breakthrough. From that point on, I studied everything I could about Bowie—and Jo Ann Donnigan. I learned that she wanted to be an actress, that her favorite Broadway musical was *Pippin*, that she liked onions on her pizza, that she drove her parents' Dodge Dart, that she wore Charlie fragrance by Revlon, that she'd had a summer job at an arts and crafts supply store, and that she'd once taken tap dance lessons. She had a thing for guys with sideburns, and she dated only athletes on the high school sports teams.

I learned most of this from a friend of hers named Lizzie Clark, who was willing to gather the information after I helped her study for a chemistry test. Lizzie had acne and a serious overbite and not many boys paid attention to her. When she got a B on that test, she ran up to me after school and kissed me on the cheek. She said "Thanks for helping me" and I said "No problem" and she said "I like you, Alfie" and I reflexively said "I like you, too, Lizzie." But I think she got the wrong idea because after that she never stopped seeking me out and touching me flirtatiously and asking if I wanted to go to Burger King on the way home from school. This one time I took her up on it, I made a joke, which made her laugh so hard she spit up her soda through her nostrils. Then she blurted out, "OK, you know I have a crush on you, right?"

That was the first time anyone had uttered those words in my direction. Sadly, I wasn't interested in Lizzie. But with her help, I was able to learn a ton about Jo Ann Donnigan—even though Lizzie often asked, "Why are you so obsessed with this girl? She thinks you're a dweeb!" Eventually, I had enough information to test Wesley's hypothesis. *Only do the stuff she liked.* My plan was to jump back in time to before we ever spoke and get her to like me by becoming her perfect match.

Such was my dedication to this love experiment that I traveled all the way back to the summer before my junior year and began practicing basketball four hours every day. Although I had the height, I was never too interested in the game—until Jo Ann became my motivation. I drilled lay-ups, jump shots, dribbling behind my back. I forced my way into pickup games to get used to the banging, rebounding, and jockeying for position.

"Again, with the basketball?" my father asked when he'd see me heading out.

"I like it," I said.

"You could like a summer job, too, you know."

"Yeah, Dad. Gotta go."

That summer I also grew what I could of sideburns—not much, but something. When school started, I tried out for the varsity team and, thanks to my summer's worth of dedication, I made the cut, which afforded me the right to wear a jacket that read JENNINGS BASKETBALL.

In our first game of the year, the opposing team heaved

a long pass over my head in the final seconds and their best shooter threw up a prayer to beat us. Afterward, I noticed Jo Ann in the stands. I wiped away my sweat and immediately transported back to that last play. This time, anticipating the pass, I stepped in front, intercepted it, and dribbled the other way for a game winning lay-up. The gym erupted with applause.

The next morning, donning my jacket, I sat down next to Jo Ann in homeroom and, without looking at her, softly sang the lyrics, "Rebel Rebel, your face is a mess . . ."

"You like Bowie?" she said.

I glanced her way and saw, for this first time, a spark of interest in her eyes.

"Love him," I said.

"Look."

She held up her notebook with the album cover image.

"Nice," I said, then I looked away, as if I'd given her enough of my attention. I slumped in the chair, feigning boredom, hoping she was staring at my sideburns.

"You played good in the game yesterday," she said.

"Oh yeah?" I replied. "Were you there?"

Now this may all sound like stupid high school stuff, Boss. But can I tell you? It worked. Eventually, Jo Ann Donnigan agreed to go out with me. We took her Dodge Dart to the movies. *The Great Gatsby* was playing. Midway through the film, after whispering, "I wish I could meet Robert Redford one day," she hooked her pinky finger around mine. It made me shiver. I turned my head her way and she flipped toward me, and next thing I knew she was planting a wet kiss on my mouth, and then another and another. It was clear she had done this many times before, while I was way out of control, like a car with no brakes on a slippery road. She put a hand on my cheek, and I figured I should do the same, except I had to cross her arm to do that, which tangled us up momentarily. I was getting dizzy from the whole encounter when she abruptly spun back to the screen—a close-up of Redford made her lose interest in my mouth—and I sucked in the deepest breath I'd ever taken and turned to blow it out.

"I like him better with a mustache," she whispered.

I came home that night feeling older, cooler. I even studied my reflection to see if there was any trace of Robert Redford in my looks. (Sadly, not a bit.)

Yet, for all the work I put in with Jo Ann Donnigan, the romance didn't last long. Two weeks later, I walked into school joking around with Wesley and I caught her glaring. Wesley took off as I slid alongside her.

"Why do you hang out with that guy?" she grumbled.

"Wes?"

"Yeah."

"What's wrong with him?"

Her voice lowered. "He's *Black*."

"So?"

"So? You know they're not the same as us."

"Come on. He's my friend."

She shook her head and made an "*Uch*" sound.

I watched her walk away, the euphoria over having made out with this beautiful girl evaporating like steam off a forgotten teacup. I felt hollow. Even a little evil. I thought about tapping out of that moment and going back a day to avoid the whole conversation. But what would that change? I knew how she felt deep down. And even if I never heard her say it out loud, it ruined everything.

I sat in class that morning realizing I had just relived almost a year of my life preparing to love a girl who now repelled me. Good Lord. What a waste.

*

Still, as useless as that experiment proved, the most puzzling discovery didn't concern the once unreachable Jo Ann Donnigan but rather the all-too-available Lizzie Clark. On my second time around, I again helped with her chemistry test, but I avoided her the day she had run up and kissed me. I never said I liked her. And I never shared that soda when she confessed her crush.

Months later, after things fell apart with Jo Ann, I ran into Lizzie after school.

"How are you doing?" I asked.

"OK, Alfie," she said. "What's up?"

"Nothing."

"Still going out with Jo Ann?"

"No. Didn't work out."

"Too bad."

I shrugged. "You want to go to Burger King?"

"Nah," she said. "I'm not hungry."

She looked across the street and waved at some friends.

"Gotta go," she said.

I watched her run off. She had zero interest in me. I couldn't understand what had happened.

A few years later, I would.

NASSAU

"OK, now you got me curious," LaPorta said. "Why'd the ugly girl turn on you?"

"She wasn't ugly."

"You said she had acne and an overbite."

"She did."

"So why'd she change?"

Alfie shifted in his chair. "I told you I'd gone back to redo my junior year."

"Yeah. To try and impress the hot one. Jo Ann."

"That's right."

"And?"

"I discovered my gift has a limit."

"What kind of limit?"

"The kind that changes the equation."

"You gonna tell me, or make me guess?"

Alfie tapped his fingers on the notebook's open page. LaPorta grimaced.

"Yeah. I know. It's all in there. I don't really care. Just hurry up."

THE COMPOSITION BOOK

Now, as I mentioned, Boss, Wesley was older than me. He didn't tell anyone for a long time, and most kids just assumed he was the same age as the rest of the class. But he had turned eighteen before our senior year started and sometime in early October he stopped coming to school. I went to his house and found him packing a duffel bag.

"What are you doing?"

"I joined the Marines."

"Why?"

"They'll pay for me to go to college. And I want to get it over with."

"What about high school?"

"I already have enough credits to graduate."

No surprise. Wesley was always taking extra classes, going over the summer. He was miles ahead of the rest of us.

"But won't you have to go to Vietnam?"

"Nah. They're not sending guys there anymore. I'll just get trained somewhere. In two years, I'm done, and college is covered."

I looked at him, speechless. Although we'd been best friends since we were kids, there had always been an older-brother vibe between Wesley and me. He had it so together. I hadn't given a realistic thought to life after high school. And here he was, packing for the military, having already solved the college tuition issue.

I asked when he was leaving. He said his parents were taking him to the Thirtieth Street train station that Sunday.

"Can I come?"

"Sure. Just don't be late."

I had to work at my part-time job that Saturday (mopping at a Kentucky Fried Chicken restaurant), but I was there the next morning at the station with Wesley's parents. I watched his mother tear up when she said goodbye. I watched his father do the firm handshake thing. I thought about trying to change that moment, to somehow keep him from leaving. But it was Wesley's path. His choice. I gave him an awkward hug before he got on the train, and he grinned and said, "See you in two years."

That night I felt so alone that I mumbled *twice* and traveled back to Saturday morning, called in sick to work, and hung out all day with Wesley. We shot baskets and ate cheesesteaks and listened to The Meters' "Just Kissed My Baby," bopping our heads to the funky bass line. We took his dad's car and drove to the Schuylkill River, where Wesley, proving his readiness for basic training, dropped into the grass and did ninety push-ups while wearing his winter coat. There was a pack of his dad's cigarettes in the glove compartment and we smoked a couple, just to feel older. We looked out at the brownish-blue water as we tried to blow smoke rings. I was really glad I'd gone back for the day.

"Don't do anything stupid in the Marines, all right?" I said.

"Like what?" Wesley said.

"Like get shot at."

"Nah. I told you. I'll be behind a desk or something."

But that's not what happened.

*

Wesley, no surprise, excelled at basic training and was already on an officer track three months into his stay. In early 1975, he came home for a weekend. He looked so much older. His hair was shaved, and his body was as thickly muscled as a gymnast's. We went for some Italian panzerottis, and he told me a story about his drill instructor.

"They're not supposed to hit the new guys, right? But this DI, he's a mean bastard. He didn't like the way one private was looking at him so he told him to stand up straight—'Like this!' he goes—and then he bangs him in the face with the butt of his rifle! And he got away with it!"

Wesley shook his head. "These military guys are crazy."

He told me he was up for two positions, one on a ship and one at a training center.

"More fun to be on a ship," I said.

"Yeah," Wesley said. Then he lowered his voice. "None of it is really fun, you know?"

He flew to San Diego the next morning. He took the ship job. I didn't hear from him for months. Then, in May, just a few weeks after the fall of Saigon, there was an incident with an American merchant vessel that was seized in international waters by Cambodia's Khmer Rouge. The Marines were sent to try and rescue it. That night at the supermarket I ran into Wesley's mother. She looked exhausted. She told me Wesley was in that unit.

"We're just praying so hard," she said. "Please pray for him, Alfie."

I said I would, but when I read the news two days later that several helicopters had been destroyed in that incident and dozens of Marines had been killed, I left prayer behind and ran to my bedroom. I flipped back through my notebooks until I found the day when Wesley had come home and, not even thinking about having to relive the last five months, I *twiced* myself back to our meal at the panzerotti shop, determined to keep him off that ship. I was so happy to see him, it must have shown on my face.

"What are you all smiles about?" he asked.

"Listen," I began. "I want to tell you something. It's a secret I've been keeping."

He pushed his glasses back on his nose.

"What?"

"I can do something other people can't."

"Drive like an idiot?"

"No."

Then, for the first time in my life, I blurted it out.

"I get to do things twice."

"What are you talking about?"

"Just what I said. I get to do things twice. If I don't like the way it first happened, I can go back and do it again. Like time travel. But only one trip."

Wesley grinned, as if trying to unwrap a riddle. "OK, go back and make Pittsburgh lose the Super Bowl. I hate those guys."

"It doesn't work like that. I can't change things I wasn't involved in."

"Oh, right." He nodded. "In that case, get Jo Ann Donnigan back as your girlfriend."

"Wes." I exhaled. "That's how I got her in the first place."

I tried explaining. The summer of basketball. The sideburns. The information from Lizzie.

"Man," he said, marveling, "you really thought this one out, didn't you?"

I dropped my head. I wasn't selling it, and he wasn't buying it. I realized this whole thing is a lot harder to explain face-to-face than it is to write down.

"Look, the reason I'm telling you this is to save your life."

"Come on, Alf—"

"I'm serious. You have a choice coming up between two jobs, a ship or a training center, right?"

He paused, then grinned.

"You got that from my mom. Nice try."

"Take the training center job."

"Alfie, stop screwing around—"

"You have a drill sergeant. You hate him. He hit one of your guys in the face with a rifle butt."

Wesley's mouth dropped.

"How do you know that?"

"Because we've been here before, Wes. We've sat at this

table. We've had this talk. When the panzerotti comes, you're gonna burn the roof of your mouth with the first bite.

"And about five months from now, if you don't take the training center job, you're gonna get sent to rescue an American cargo vessel on the island of Koh Tang and a lot of people are going to die."

"Where the hell is Koh Tang?"

"Cambodia."

I saw him swallow. His voice dropped to a whisper.

"What happens to *me*?"

"I don't know. All I know is it's really dangerous. I came back to warn you."

I looked at Wes's hands. They were trembling. I leaned in closer.

"Just take the training center job, OK?"

*

Now what I didn't tell Wesley was that even if he did what I said, I couldn't assure his survival. I learned this from my mother in our last conversation together:

"Alfie, don't try to go back and save me," she said. "I'll always die when I'm supposed to die. You can't undo it."

"Why?"

"That's just how this power is."

"How do you know?"

"Because I had it, too."

"Then why don't you save yourself, Mom?"

"I did save myself. That's why we came to Africa."

"I don't understand."

"I had another life, Alfie, a different life, before this one. It was more selfish. I was losing my heart and my soul. So I went back and changed things. I put other people's problems ahead of mine. I was a better mother to you. A better wife to your father. And I was happier."

She sighed. "I just didn't know it would be so short."

I was lost. I leaned into her and felt her arms drape tightly around me.

"Mom?"

"Yes, my angel?"

"I don't want you to go."

She brushed my face with her fingers. "I want, and you want, and God does what God wants."

*

I thought about that conversation after seeing Wesley at the panzerotti shop. Two days later, he went back to his unit and took the training center job. And I lived through the next five months like a convict in a dark cell, not knowing if the executioner was coming.

When the incident started with the Cambodians overseas, I called Wes every day at his office. He was fine. But on the day they released the names of the dead Marines, I called him again. No answer.

That night, at our house, the phone rang and my father picked it up. I saw his expression change. My stomach sank. When he held out the receiver, I already knew what was coming.

"It's Wesley's mother," he said softly. "There's been an accident."

NASSAU

"Whoa, what are you saying?" LaPorta interrupted. "He died anyhow?"

"Yes." Alfie looked away. "I never had another friend like him."

"How'd it happen?"

"An explosion at the training center. Wes was in the basement, trying to fix a boiler, and something blew up. A freak accident. No one else was hurt."

"And you think that was because of what you did?"

"Not because of it. Despite it."

"Come on. It was a coincidence. The guy was ten thousand miles from Cambodia."

Alfie shook his head. "It's not where, it's *when*. Wesley died when he was fated to die. I dug around until I found the exact time of his accident, then researched when the Marines got attacked."

"Don't tell me. They were the same."

Alfie nodded.

"I don't buy it," LaPorta scoffed. "Stuff just happens. Especially in the military."

"You served?"

"Army. Late '90s. Got out just before Iraq. I was lucky."

"Luck had nothing to do with it."

"Says the guy who cheated a casino."

Alfie paused.

"Suspicion and belief—"

"Can't share the same bed. Yeah, yeah, I know. It's a load of crap. Read."

THE COMPOSITION BOOK

My high school graduation was a few weeks later. It was a hot day and half the kids didn't wear pants under their gowns. They'd asked me to say a few words about Wesley, who was being given a diploma in absentia, but I didn't want to be out there in front of everybody and maybe tearing up, so I declined. Instead, the school's vice principal read a statement. It was really short, and he mispronounced Wesley's last name. I glanced at Wesley's parents, who had come at the school's invitation, and saw his mom look at her feet. It made me so furious that I tapped out in the middle of the ceremony and went back two weeks to the moment they asked me. This time I said yes. The trip backward meant I had to take all my final exams again, which was a pain. But I couldn't live with the idea that my best friend's final high school mention was a botched pronunciation.

"Wesley was a really great guy," I said at graduation. "He was super smart and super nice and sometimes he seemed a lot older than he was. He took time before he said stuff, but when he finally spoke, you were like, 'Wow, I never thought of that.' He was brave to go into the Marines, braver than most of us. Braver than me. Not everybody here in school knew him, but if you had, you would have really liked him . . . You would have loved him . . ."

I choked up on the word *loved* and wobbled through my last few lines. But afterward, Wesley's mother found me and, holding a tissue to her eyes, whispered, "He would have clapped for what you said." That made me feel better. Even Jo Ann Donnigan came up and told me she was sorry I had lost my friend. Then she kissed me hard on the lips. It was one of those moments that, if you'd offered me a million dollars, I still wouldn't know what to say. People are so unpredictable.

*

A year later my father announced we were taking a trip to Florida, to see the new Disney World they had opened up down there. He could tell I wasn't enjoying life after high school. He had wanted me to go to college, but I was in a funk after Wesley died and never finished the applications, so I took a job with a plumbing company and buried myself in it. I wasn't very good, but they paired me with a kindly old plumber named Bernie Schneider who'd show me everything I'd done wrong. Then I'd tap back an hour earlier and do it correctly.

"How come you were so good with sink pipes, but you can't figure out a toilet?" Bernie would say. Didn't matter. I'd get the toilet right the second time.

During this stretch, I often used my second-chance power to break up my boredom. Sometimes, on the way to work, I would turn the car around, drive to the airport, and use my father's credit card for a ticket to somewhere cool—California, Montana, Texas. Once there, I'd search for something dangerous to try. Diving off a cliff. Galloping on a horse. In Austin, I took a skydiving lesson with three other people. While the instructor was checking everyone's parachutes, I raced past him and jumped out the plane's open door. I remember the crazy noise of the wind, the floating sensation, and how surprisingly cold it was. I closed my eyes and thought, *How many seconds before I die?* And then–*whumpf!* The instructor (who had jumped out in pursuit) had his arms around me and his helmet pressing into my neck and I heard him screaming "What the hell are you doing?" and I yelled "*Twice!*" and was back on the highway the day before, driving to my plumbing job. No flight to Texas. No charge on my dad's credit card. No angry jump instructor. And no one to share the story with.

Looking back, I suppose I was depressed. I had lost Wesley as I had lost my mother. Both too young. Both too soon. Perhaps dallying with death was a way of feeling closer to where they'd gone. I don't know. It doesn't always make sense, the way you miss somebody. Sometimes, hurt seeks hurt.

*

Anyhow, my dad and I were in the car heading to Florida, and somewhere around North Carolina, he started pushing college again.

"You need a degree to get a good job."

"Yeah."

"You don't want to be a plumber the rest of your life, do you?"

"No."

"It's been a year, Alfie. What do you want to do?"

I wanted to say music, which was the only thing that really interested me. But with my father, there were only two acceptable answers. Lawyer or accountant. *People will always be suing each other,* he would say, *and they'll always need to count their money. Steady work. That's what you want, Alfie.*

"I don't know, Dad," I said.

"You *still* don't know?"

"I'm *sorry.*" I exhaled in frustration. "What did *you* want to do when you were my age?"

He shifted his hands on the wheel. His voice dropped.

"I wanted to be an opera singer."

I did a double take. "Really?"

I knew my father had a good voice. It was deep and resonant, and when my mother was still alive, he would sing to her now and then. Sometimes, when he'd reach the end of the song, he'd spread his arms out wide and get really loud, and I swear I could see his voice bounce from one wall to the other. He did this once when we lived in Mombasa, and when he finished singing, there were five villagers at our door, asking if everything was all right.

"Don't act so surprised," he said, staring straight ahead. "I knew my stuff. I listened to Beniamino Gigli. And Björling. I even took lessons for a while with a man who'd met Caruso."

"So you were good?"

"I wasn't bad."

"Why didn't you do it then?"

"What?"

"Become an opera singer."

He glared at me.

"Something called World War II, remember?"

I looked down at my feet. I knew my father had fought in the South Pacific. Infantry division. He didn't talk about it much.

"But what about after the war?" I said, softly. "Couldn't you have been an opera singer then?"

"After the war, things were different."

"Oh."

I paused. Perhaps I'd miscalculated my father's disapproval of the arts.

"You know," I said, "maybe I could study music at college?"

"Don't be stupid, Alfie," he said.

*

We never did see Disney World. My father drove there, took one look at the massive line of vehicles trying to enter the parking lot and grumbled, "You've got to be kidding me." He turned the car around and headed south. He wasn't the most patient man in the world.

We wound up driving four more hours, all the way to Miami, with me staring out an open window, hot wind blowing on my face. I was thinking about Wesley, which made me quiet, and I guess my dad thought I was upset about skipping the Magic Kingdom, which I wasn't.

"Tell you what," he said when we reached the Miami city

limits. "Let's go to the zoo. They have a big zoo here. What do you think?"

What I thought was, *The zoo? What am I, five years old?*

What I said was, "Yeah, sure."

I had no idea how that trip would change my life.

*

There are years you think about for moments, and moments you think about for years. What happened next is a moment that never leaves my heart.

I entered that zoo bored, hot, and grimy. My father found a little pavilion where they served beer, and he sat down to drink one. I wandered around. The zoo was in lousy shape. Apparently, they'd endured a hurricane and never fully recovered.

I meandered past a small reptile house badly in need of paint, and a monkey village where I didn't see any monkeys. I passed a weary-looking mother pushing two kids in a double stroller, and heard them scream at the sight of a pink flamingo. I thought back to the time I'd scaled a wall to face a lion. It seemed so pointless now. Nobody knew I'd done it but me, and nobody truly knew me at all. The one person I had shared my secret with was gone.

I was shaken from these thoughts by a sudden blast of noise. I recognized it immediately: an elephant's trumpet. I moved in that direction until I saw its dark gray outline shifting behind some trees. When I got closer, the elephant emerged in full view. From the size of its tusks, it seemed fairly young, and from the angle of its forehead I guessed it was female. It stared at me for a few long moments, and I smiled, as if trying to be friendly, which was dumb.

Then I heard another sound. Clicking. Rapid clicking.

I turned to my right and saw, about thirty feet away, a young woman shooting a long-lensed camera. She wore a purple tank top and denim shorts. She had a second camera around her neck, and I figured she was getting some elephant photos. But when I glanced again, it seemed her camera was pointed at me.

I stepped back from the railing to make sure I was right. Sure enough, she shifted in my direction.

I took a few steps closer as she adjusted her lens. I still couldn't see who she was. Finally, I yelled out, "Hey, what are you doing?"

"It is you, isn't it?" she yelled back.

"Who?"

"Alfie?"

I recoiled.

"How do you know my name?"

"Come on."

"Come on, what?"

"Lallu!"

"Lallu?" I mumbled.

She lowered the camera, and I blinked at the sight of the loveliest face I would ever encounter. Full lips. Voluminous black hair that fell over her forehead and shoulders. Cheeks that pushed all the way up into her green eyes when she smiled, and a smile so welcoming it sent little lightning bolts into my skin. For the first time in a long time, whatever funk or depression or ennui I was suffering evaporated. It wasn't that she was so beautiful, but rather, after all these years, still so familiar.

"Princess?"

She threw her head back and laughed.

"I haven't heard that name since I was eight years old."

She moved toward me then, her cameras swaying across her torso, and held out her hand like a queen.

"My actual name is Gianna," she said. "Gianna Rule."

"I'm Alfie," I rasped.

"I know," she said.

NASSAU

"Finally!" LaPorta declared. "We meet the mystery woman! Now I gotta pee."

He rose to his feet. "By the way, they'll be here shortly."

"Who?" Alfie asked.

"The police. That's how it works. They give me a little time to try and get to the bottom of things, then they take you to jail and see if that shakes a confession out of you."

He paused. "Jails aren't great here. Just so you know."

LaPorta hoped for a reaction, but Alfie simply exhaled. *This guy*, the detective thought, *what's it gonna take to shake him?*

The truth was, the evidence they had against Alfie was circumstantial. He had won three straight roulette plays, each time betting a single number, the highest payoff with the longest odds. He'd cashed out immediately and had gone to a bank to make a wire transfer. The next morning, the police had caught up with him outside a travel agency where he'd been buying tickets to Africa. Suspicious, yes. But so far, no proof of illegality.

LaPorta had never seen anyone hit a single roulette number more than once in a night, much less three times in a row. The only explanation was rigging the wheel itself, or a scam involving the croupier, who had been picked up and was, at this very moment, being interrogated in another room, now that LaPorta's Bahamian cohorts had finally arrived.

He privately hoped the croupier would implicate Alfie, although he had to admit, the notebook *was* entertaining. More fun than the typical "I swear I didn't do it!" LaPorta remembered a quote he'd read during his training. *People will forgive you anything but boredom.* This Alfie guy was anything but boring.

"I'll be back in a minute," LaPorta said. "Then you can tell me where to find Gianna Rule."

"She had nothing to do with the roulette winnings."

"Right," LaPorta said, stepping out. "Don't go anywhere."

He locked the door behind him.

"Where would I go?" he heard Alfie say.

THE COMPOSITION BOOK

Things my mother said she loved about me:

5. "The way you remember every little thing that happened."

The afternoon I remet Gianna, all the other girls I had liked, dreamed about, or made a fool of myself in front of suddenly moved behind the clouds. She was the only star in the sky. We spoke for more than an hour by that elephant exhibit, leaning on the railing, shifting positions, finding a bench, shifting again. There was a rhythm to our conversation that felt like old music. She asked. I answered. I asked. She answered. Her family had left Kenya eight years earlier and moved to Morocco, then Italy, then the Philippines, where her mother was from, now America, all because of her father's work. She said at times she felt like a "Tuareg nomad," two words I'd never heard anyone use to describe themselves. She was hoping to stay put for a while by going to college at Boston University, where she planned to study literature. But mostly she wanted to be a photographer. I kept staring at her lips. Her teeth. Her eyes.

"What do you want to take pictures of?" I asked.

"Wildlife. Natural habitats."

She grinned. "Old boyfriends."

"Come on," I said. "I wasn't really your boyfriend."

"I didn't mean you."

I felt myself turning crimson.

"Oh . . . I . . ."

"Ha. Look at your face!" She laughed again with that perfect smile and rapped my arm with her fist.

"Sorry," I said.

"Don't be sorry. Weren't we going to get married one day and buy a house in Mombasa?"

"You remember that?"

"Yep. I'm like her." She nodded to the elephant. "I never forget."

*

When I finally got back to my father, there were four empty beer cans on the table and he'd unbuttoned his shirt due to the heat.

"Where the hell did you go?" he barked.

"I was checking out the elephants."

He shook his head, exasperated. *"Elephants?"*

"Yeah."

"To wait this long, I could have stayed in Disney World."

"Sorry."

He looked away, his face scrunched in anger.

"Hey, Dad?"

"What?"

"I've been thinking. Maybe I do want to go to college."
His expression changed. So did his voice.
"Oh, yeah? Well. Good."
Then he asked, "Where?"
"Boston," I said.

Three

THE COMPOSITION BOOK

I've noticed something about dying, Boss. When you come into this world, you have all these people who want to take care of you, and you don't know any of them. Then, when you're leaving this world, you have all these people you *do* know, but few of them want to be bothered.

I went to a facility last week. It was recommended by my doctor. Plenty of windows. Good light. But sad. Sad in that dreary, dragging manner of old folks' homes, with their carpeted hallways and low-volume conversations and lingering smells from the last meal cooked, like fried fish or macaroni and cheese.

I'll be heading there soon. I have no choice. This disease I have will render me immobile and noncommunicative. They'll keep me fed and hydrated (sounds like a plant, now that I write it). And pretty soon, I'll be gone.

It's OK. I've accepted it. To be honest, I think I'll miss walking more than talking. The only person I enjoy speaking to anymore is you.

I hope that doesn't embarrass you, Boss. This all ties back to the story. You see, before we left Florida, my father and I went to visit my grandmother in a nursing home, much like the one where I'll soon be heading. It was in a town called Hollywood, which I expected to look like the California version. It did not. Back in the 1970s, Hollywood, Florida, was a sprawl of ranch homes, palm trees, a pink-cement ocean promenade, and an Indian reservation.

My mother's Mom, Nina—who I always called "Yaya Nina"—was born in Greece but immigrated to America with her family when she was young. She grew up in the Florida heat and, the story goes, married the first man to ever take her to an air-conditioned movie theater, my grandpa Billy. They moved to Virginia, where he worked as a fisherman. They had one child together, my mother, and not long after she became the first in the family to go to college, Grandpa Billy died. Heart attack. I never got to meet him. He was buried at sea. Yaya Nina moved back to Florida. She never left.

Before my mom died, we used to visit Yaya a lot, but after that, there wasn't much contact beyond birthday cards and a phone call at the holidays. The last time I'd seen Yaya was at my mother's funeral. She'd stayed at our house and baked me shortbread cookies filled with orange jam. At one point we were in the kitchen together—she was smoking, which she often did—and she said something curious. She was holding one of the framed photos we had put around the house, a picture of my mom in Kenya, reading the Bible to the village kids.

"She didn't have to go all the way to Africa, you know," she said.

"What do you mean?"

"She could have helped people here."

I thought about that. Maybe if she had stayed in America, she would still be alive. This was before I understood that all the magic in the world couldn't delay death.

"Did you ever tell her that, Yaya?" I asked.

"No." She looked away. "But I will."

*

It was my idea to visit Yaya Nina, seeing as we were in Miami and so close. My dad agreed without much fuss, I'm guessing because he was happy about my college news.

"She might not recognize you," he warned.

"Why not?"

"It's been eleven years. I don't know what kind of shape she's in."

We had to look up the facility in the phone book. It was a single-level, red brick structure, with pale green carpet and easy-listening music playing over the speakers. We asked for my grandmother at the front desk. When they brought her out, she was in a wheelchair, and since we hadn't called ahead, I thought she'd be surprised to see us. But she quickly took my hand and smiled, causing her face to wrinkle into so many lines, it seemed as if she were drawn with an Etch A Sketch. Her cheekbones nearly pushed through her tanned skin, and her straight hair, silver and white, still hung over her forehead in bangs. Her grip was strong.

"You, I want to talk to," she told me, ignoring my dad.

She motioned the orderly to take us down the hall, and I looked back at my father, who nodded as if to say, *Do as she wants.* We left him in the lobby, went to her room together, and started talking.

That conversation changed everything.

*

"You got big," she said.

"Yeah."

"Very tall now."

"I guess."

"And what are you going to do with your life?"

"I don't know. I like music."

"Mmm. Like your mother."

She pointed to a glass of water, which I retrieved from her bureau. She took a long sip, then put the glass down so deliberately, you'd have thought it contained explosives.

"So, Alfie," she said. "Got any cigarettes?"

"Yaya!" I laughed. "They let you smoke in here?"

"Of course, not. That's why I asked."

She ran her gaze up and down my body. I remembered as a child feeling that whenever she looked at me, there was something she wasn't saying. I felt that way now.

"You have to understand," she suddenly blurted out, "I was very angry at your father! Keeping us apart all these years! Last time I saw you, you were a child. Now look! Look at what I missed! Terrible!"

Her voice rose to a frustrated pitch. "I shouldn't have screamed at him. But I couldn't help it! I was mad!"

"When did you scream at him?"

"Just now. When you came in."

"Yaya," I said softly, "you didn't say a word to him."

She waved her fingers dismissively.

"The first time. I reamed him out pretty good."

"What are you talking about?"

She stared straight at me, boring her eyes into mine. I felt myself shiver. Then, as if finishing a test, she relaxed and leaned back.

"You know what I'm talking about."

She grinned.

"You can do it, too."

*

It turned out, Boss, that my grandmother had the same power as me. So did her brother and her father, she said. There was no explanation, other than it seemed to pass from a loved one just before they died, as if knowing, with death looming, that it needed a new host.

"When was your first time?" Yaya asked me.

"Mom's last day."

"You saw that twice?"

"Yes."

She nodded and looked to the window. "Makes sense. It's usually a heartbreak that starts it. You want so badly to undo something. And then . . . it just happens."

She shrugged. "Your mother's power must have passed to you, just like my father's passed to me."

"Are we the only people in the world who can do this?"

"I don't know anyone else. Do you?"

"Yaya, I didn't know *you* could do it until just now."

"Yes, well." She clasped her hands together. "Now you do."

"When was your first time?" I asked.

She hesitated.

"When I was ten, just after my father passed away."

"What caused it?"

"There was this old man in our neighborhood. Always wore a brown suit and hat. One day, when my mother went to the grocery store, he came by the house. I was alone. He asked if I liked chocolate cake. He said he would give me some if I did something for him."

"What?"

"Something a young girl should never be asked to do."

"Oh, no."

She looked down. "Before he could touch me, I ran out the door. I hid in the trees all day, crying and wishing I had gone with my mother. I fell asleep on the ground. When I woke up, it was morning again and I was back in bed. Same clothes. Same breakfast. I thought I was dreaming. This time I went to the store and held my mother's arm. I screamed when she tried to let go."

"Did you ever see that man again?"

"Once, a few years later. I was with my friends at the boardwalk. He walked by in his brown suit and I pointed and started yelling, 'Creeper! Creeper!' He ran away."

"Wow," I said.

"Yes."

"And after that, did you start time jumping?"

"Oh, eventually, yes. I did many things over. Not so much anymore."

She leaned in. Her voice lowered.

"Alfie?"

"Uh-huh?"

"Have you told your father?"

"No."

She leaned back. "Better that way."

"I guess."

We sat there in the hung silence that follows a confession. I suddenly felt so connected to my grandmother. I also realized I had just taken part in one of her time jumps, and had no idea what had happened the first go-around, except that she'd yelled at my father. So this was what it felt like for everyone I had affected that way. It felt like . . . nothing.

She tried to change the mood. She tapped my thigh.

"So. You got a girlfriend?"

"Not really . . . There's this one girl."

"Tell me."

"Not much to tell."

"You love her?"

"Come on, Yaya."

"What?"

"We haven't even gone out yet."

"Well." She straightened her dress in her lap. "Just be careful."

"What do you mean?"

"Your power. It's very tempting with love. You'll think you can make everything perfect." She grabbed my hand. "You can't, OK? You understand?"

"Yes, Yaya."

She released her grip. Her shoulders drooped.

"I'm tired, Alfie. I didn't know you were coming. You should call next time, so I can drink some coffee before you get here." She looked toward the door. "Call for the nurse. I want to get back into bed."

"Wait, Yaya—"

There was so much more I wanted to know.

"Why do we only get to go back once?" I asked.

She scratched her head, then looked at her fingers.

"I really wish I had a cigarette."

"Yaya, did you hear me? Why do we only get to go back once?"

She sighed, as if it were obvious.

"Alfie, if you keep getting second chances, you won't learn a damn thing."

NASSAU

"Miss me?" LaPorta said, reentering the room.

"Everything all right?" Alfie said.

"Yep. Had to pee, that's all."

LaPorta had actually been checking with his partners. The results were not promising. The croupier, under questioning, had denied any involvement. And the video of Alfie's winnings only showed him sitting down at the roulette table and stacking his chips early on those single numbers. A cheat wouldn't do that. He would more likely wait until late in the roll, lay several bets, or skip a roll to throw off suspicion. Alfie had looked relaxed, casual. Only on the third number did he seem to hesitate, before pushing all his chips on 28 black. Since he'd been building his stack with each success, that was the biggest payout. More than two million dollars. He gathered his winnings, rose from his chair, and cashed out.

LaPorta was certain others were in on it. But the croupier insisted he'd never seen Alfie before. His colleagues from the casino were now being questioned. Meanwhile, LaPorta had only Alfie's wild notebook story to work with. *Keep him talking. Maybe he'll slip up.*

"So where were we?"

"Gianna Rule," Alfie said.

"Right. Your beneficiary."

"Excuse me?"

"The bank transfer? The money?"

"Ah. Yes. The money."

"*Ah, yes, the money*," LaPorta mocked. "What'd you think I was talking about?"

THE COMPOSITION BOOK

Things my mother said she loved about me:

6. "The way you get down on the floor to explore the small things."

I went to college for love. That's the truth of it. Every step at Boston University, from picking my classes to moving into the dormitories to buying the books to waiting in line at the dining halls, was all in hopes of being with Gianna. Our reunion at the zoo had sparked an attraction I'd never felt before. I needed to see where it went.

Of course, she didn't know any of this. And with almost twenty thousand undergraduates milling about, finding her took some effort. The student directory had only her photo, no housing information. She wasn't at the orientation events. I even went to the first meeting of the photography club, hoping she'd show up.

It would have been easier—much easier—if I'd traveled back to that day in Miami and asked Gianna for a phone number, which I'd stupidly neglected to do. But that encounter was one of my favorite memories, and I didn't want to risk changing any of it.

So I spent mornings hanging outside dormitories and afternoons walking laps in the cafeterias. I even snuck into freshman literature classes to search for her. Some of those lecture halls were so large that I just walked to the front of the room and shouted, "Excuse me! Is Gianna Rule in here?" Everyone stared, but what did I care? Once I saw she wasn't, I tapped out and tried another class. I even thumbtacked large notes with my dorm phone number on the community poster boards, under the words: GIANNA RULE: CALL ALFIE. Still no luck.

Then one night I went for a swim at the university's indoor pool. About twenty minutes into it, I noticed a woman doing laps alongside me. I thought I saw her look at me and wave, but it happened so fast that I couldn't be sure.

I tried to keep up, but she was a much faster swimmer, so I waited until she passed me going the other direction. Sure enough, she waved again. She was Gianna's size and shape. But because she wore a bathing cap and goggles, I barely got a glimpse of her face. Still, it had to be her. Who else would be signaling me?

I made the turn, flipped around, and anticipated her coming my way. But the lane was suddenly empty.

I rose to the surface, gasping air, and spotted her walking toward the locker rooms. I slapped through several lanes, nearly smashing into a guy doing the backstroke, and yanked myself out of the pool. From behind, her body looked more curvy than I remembered it. Just before I caught up, she pulled her swim cap off to reveal a mop of red hair. Then, whoever this woman was looked at me and shook her head, as if I were pathetic. She disappeared into the women's locker room.

I turned to go, dripping, totally embarrassed, when I heard a familiar voice.

"I was right. A guy will follow any girl who waves at him."

I spun to see Gianna, in a green bathing suit and shower togs. The redhead stepped out behind her. They both grinned.

"This is my friend, Laura," Gianna said. She put her hands on her hips. "So. I hear you've been looking for me."

*

You know that expression "bowled over"? That's how I constantly felt around Gianna back then. From that moment at the pool onward, every encounter, every brief conversation, left me off-balance. Being able to do things twice may have sharpened my confidence with other people, but around her I felt awkward in how I stood, how I slouched, even where I put my arms. It was as if my body were constantly auditioning. They say the strongest kinds of love make you feel that way, right? Sort of dizzy? I was dizzy around Gianna all the time.

Still we never started a relationship. Quite the opposite. A few weeks later, I saw her on the campus lawn, lying on a blanket, reading a book. She wore a cropped blue top and tight yellow shorts. Some shirtless guys were playing soccer on the nearby grass, and Gianna was watching as I stepped up behind her. I couldn't help but stare at her bare, tanned legs as she loosely kicked them up and down, her small feet moving like flippers.

"You know it's creepy to stare at a girl's butt," she said. She spun her head around. "You're not a creep, are you, Alfie?"

I felt a flame of embarrassment shoot up my spine. As her eyes locked on mine, I actually *yelled* the word "*Twice!*" and was instantly back in my earlier class, breathing so hard, the guy next to me whispered, "Hey, man, are you all right?"

"Yeah, yeah," I said. "Fine."

When class ended, I exited the building and reminded myself that Gianna knew none of my previous behavior. I saw her again on the lawn. I took a deep breath. This time I approached from the front, determined to be aloof. I stared at a book as I passed by her.

"Hey, Alfie," she yelled. "What are you reading?"

I looked up as innocently as I could fake it.

"Oh. Hey, Gianna."

"What's the book?"

I had to flip it over. I didn't even know.

"*The Divided Self.*"

"Any good?"

"You know. So-so. It's for sociology so I—"

She turned away to smile at someone, one of the shirtless soccer players who was jogging her way. He had thick black hair and dark stubble on his cheeks. He dropped to his knees and kissed Gianna on the forehead while resting a hand on the small of her back, just above the yellow shorts that had gotten me in trouble minutes earlier.

"Hey, Alfie, do you know Mike?" Gianna said.

"Hey, man," Mike said, smiling. His teeth were perfect.

"*Twice,*" I mumbled under my breath. "*Twice... Twice...*"

But I had already redone this moment. There was no going back again.

"Hey, man," I finally croaked back, a weaker version of Mike's words, befitting a man who was obviously, to Gianna, a weaker suitor.

*

For the rest of our freshman year, I got no closer than friendship would allow. Gianna was popular with a wide swath of people who all seemed to adore her. I'd see her laughing in the student lounge with a group of Filipino classmates, or doing morning exercises with a tai chi club, or working in the cafeteria where she had a part-time job, chatting up some older kitchen staff who seemed to treat her like a peer. Whenever there were others around us, she would introduce me as "Alfie, a guy I used to ride elephants with in Africa."

Now and then, I would see her arm in arm with Mike, whose last name was Kurtz, and who, it turns out, was a star goalie on the university's soccer team. And a senior. This made me feel young and clumsy around them, and I found myself undoing so many moments—times I said something lame, or she caught me staring—that I must have added a semester's worth of second tries.

One time I was playing piano in a practice room (despite my dad's objections, I was majoring in music) and Gianna passed by the open door and saw me. I was in the middle of singing "Try Me" by James Brown, a wailing, plaintive ballad that my mother used to play on her old turntable.

> *"Try me, try me,*
> *Darling tell me, 'I need you.'"*

"Alfie?"

I stopped playing. My face went red.

"Wow, Alfie. You're really good."

I shrugged. But inside, I was happy with the compliment. I'd gotten to sing those words to Gianna without having to say them. Maybe she'd take a hint.

"Do you want to hear a song?" I asked. Then I added, "Any song?"

"You can play *any* song?"

"Try me."

She smiled. "You were just singing that. 'Try me.'"

"Yeah."

She made a deep-thought face. "OK. You'll never know this one. It's called 'Blue Room.' Ella Fitzgerald sang it. My father used to play that for my mother."

I'd never heard of it. But I zapped myself back two days, found it, studied it, and had it ready to play the second time she came down the hall and caught me singing.

"Wow, Alfie. You're really good."

"Do you want to hear a song? Any song?"

"You can play *any* song?"

"Try me."

"You were just singing that. 'Try me.'"

"Yeah."

"OK. You'll never know this one. It's called 'Blue Room'—"

"By Ella Fitzgerald?" I interrupted.

"Wow. Yeah. You've heard of it?"

"Uh-huh. I think it goes like..."

Just as I put my hands on the keys, Gianna turned her head and yelled, "Mike! Hey! Down here!"

I swallowed. Suddenly Mike appeared in the doorway. He was carrying a guitar.

"Alfie is going to play this great old song," Gianna said.

Mike smiled. "Oh yeah? Which one?"

"'Blue Room.' I love it. Go ahead, Alfie."

I looked at their happy, waiting faces. My shoulders slumped.

"I don't really know it, to be honest. I thought I did."

They stared with pasted smiles.

"Sorry," I added.

"That's OK," Gianna said. "It's really old."

A pause.

"Well. See ya later."

Off they went.

*

There were so many incidents like this that my composition book was full of dates and scribbles, a zigzag record of our encounters and reencounters. (My notebook collection was now so huge that I kept the ones from childhood at home, in boxes in the basement. I started anew at college.)

Sometimes I leafed through the pages and was taken aback at how many moments I had repeated with Gianna. I remembered what Yaya had said about love: *You'll think you can make everything perfect. You can't.* I wondered if this was what she meant.

I tried getting to know other girls, Boss. I had two roommates. One of them, Elliot, was a good-looking guy in the theater program who felt sorry for me and would drag me to parties where he chatted up women, then brought me into the conversation. I tried to engage with them. I really did. But within minutes I would start comparing them to Gianna, and they always fell short. No chemistry. Not as funny. Not as compelling. It seems silly, I know, dismissing potential romances because they didn't match a fantasy. What was I saving myself for? Gianna didn't even like me that much.

Then, one night during finals week of my freshman year, I was heading up the library steps when I saw Gianna curled on a bench. Her arms were wrapped around her knees, as if she were trying to make herself as small as possible.

"Hey, are you OK?" I said.

She glanced up quickly. Her face was tear-stained.

"What's the matter?"

"Nothing."

"Doesn't look like nothing."

"What does nothing look like?"

Even crying, she managed to throw me.

"Can I help?" I asked. "I mean . . . I want to help . . . if there's something I can . . . you know . . ."

"I'm fine, Alfie." She sniffed. "Oh, God. This is something I swore I would never do."

"What's that?"

"Cry over a guy."

I figured she meant Mike. But I didn't want to say his name.

"Yeah. OK. Well, I guess—"

"He's graduating," she blurted out. "So he decided we should break up. Just like that. He said he 'doesn't see any future in it.' Like I'm a stock or something."

She lifted her shirt collar and wiped tears off her cheek. "How does anyone know what the future is anyhow?"

I resisted the urge to tell her it was easy.

"You should leave me alone, Alfie," she said.

"Why?"

"Because I'm embarrassed."

Embarrassed? I wanted to tell her how embarrassed I felt around her constantly. How embarrassed I was that her green eyes, even crying, froze me when they flashed my way. How embarrassed I was that her voice right now, hoarse from crying, sounded so seductive I wanted to lose myself inside it.

I couldn't verbalize such thoughts. Instead, I said the only thing that would come out of my mouth:

"He's a fool."

She tilted her head and squinted, as if not sure what she just heard, and for a moment I thought, *You have to undo that, right now, go back, say twice.* But before I could, her expression melted into a soft smile, and I don't know how to describe it, except to say that I felt the earth shift.

"Alfie," she said, lightly touching my hand, "you're sweet."

And that was the start of everything.

*

As I read this over, Boss, I realize how chaste it seems. Young people today think nothing of jumping into bed the first time they meet. All those movie scenes where the couple bursts through the apartment door and slams against the wall, undressing each other in mad abandon. I'm sure it happened back in the '70s, too. But not to me. Not when I was nineteen, anyhow. Things went slower. And deep down, I sensed that when it came to Gianna, her affection would need to be earned, deliberately, meritoriously. Maybe I was just too scared to go faster.

In any case, summer came and we both went home, me to Philadelphia and Gianna to San Francisco, her father's latest transfer. But we spoke on the phone a few times, and after a month she told me she was coming to visit her roommate, who, lucky for me, lived in New Jersey, just over the bridge.

"Maybe we can hang out?" I said.

"Yeah, that would be cool," she replied.

The week she arrived, we agreed to meet on a Saturday

afternoon and go to the Philadelphia Zoo. I figured that was innocent enough. And zoos seemed to work for us.

I borrowed my father's Plymouth and picked her up at her roommate's house. I can still remember the way she bounded out the front door, in a backless blue denim dress with a white bandanna in her hair, her omnipresent camera around her neck. She smiled before she even reached the car, as if happiness were her default mode.

"Hey, stranger," she said, pulling open the door.

"Hey," I replied.

"Let's go see some elephants."

We spent the early afternoon wandering through the exhibits, eating ice cream, and giving the animals names. Gianna snapped pictures, and I asked questions about cameras, lenses, anything to keep her talking. I loved the cadence of her voice when she got excited, and her bursts of knowledge, which left me bedeviled. "Did you know llamas hum when they're happy?" "Did you know cheetahs can see three miles away?" She was so full of facts that I adopted a standard response—"I didn't know that"—until I said it so often, she started mimicking me.

"I didn't know that . . . I didn't know that," she said, deepening her voice and crossing her eyes like a broken toy. I laughed.

"You should know more things, Alfie Logan."

"I know that."

"Ha ha."

Of course, one thing I did know that Gianna did not was

how many miscues I had erased from her memory. Times I did something embarrassing or mumbled something out of jealousy. She once said to me, "Don't you ever mess up, Alfie?" and I wanted to answer, *You have no idea.* Instead, I hid my flaws, afraid they would cost me her affection.

That would prove to be a mistake, and my first lesson in The Truth About True Love: what we yearn for, deep down, is a heart that will embrace us *after* we make a fool of ourselves.

*

We stayed at the zoo until just past sunset, when the animals, having had their final feedings, began crawling off to sleep.

"We should go, I guess," I said.

She looked disappointed.

"But we're having fun."

"Yeah, we are."

"You know what my favorite time of day was in Africa, Alfie?"

"What?"

"Just after sundown, when you started to hear the noises. The insects chirping. The cuckoos and the other birds, the nightjars, the owls. Sometimes you'd hear the zebras barking."

"Why did you like that?"

"I don't know. I guess it made me feel less alone."

"You felt alone in Africa?"

She looked at me as if considering a secret.

"I feel alone most of the time."

I didn't know how to respond to that.

"Even now?" I finally said.

"Well, not *now*, Alfie," she said, laughing.

And she took my hand.

She took my hand. What an arterial burst of joy! Her palm was soft and small enough to be dwarfed by mine, and we slid our fingers sideways until they fell in place, then tightened as if snapping two souls together. We began walking to the zoo exit. We didn't say a word. But she leaned into me, and her head grazed my shoulder, and every inch of my body felt like it was smiling. Nothing in my life ever seemed as destined as that moment.

Sadly, Gianna wouldn't remember any of it.

*

When I got home that night, the house was dark, and I figured my father was asleep. I got into bed still thinking about Gianna and passed out happily a few minutes later. Next thing I knew, light was coming through the window and the phone was ringing. I was groggy and figured Dad would get it, so I rolled over and tried going back to sleep. When it kept ringing, I dragged out of bed.

"Hello?" I mumbled.

"Is this the Logan residence?"

"Uh . . . yeah?"

"This is Memorial Hospital. I'm calling about Lawrence Logan."

"My father?"

"So you're his son?"

"Yes . . . ?"

"There was an accident. We used his driver's license to find this number. We called several times during the surgery yesterday, but nobody answered."

"What surgery?"

A pause.

"It might be better if you came down. Do you have a way to get here?"

"Yes . . . I . . . I have his car . . . but—"

"We can explain everything once you get here."

"Hold on, hold on," I stammered. "Is he . . . alive?"

The words came from my mouth as if someone else were using my voice.

"Yes. He's alive. Come as soon as you can."

NASSAU

"Wait," LaPorta interrupted, "what happened to him?"

Alfie looked up from the notebook.

"If I keep reading, you'll—"

"Just tell me."

Alfie leaned back.

"He had a headache. We were out of aspirin. Since I had the car, he decided to walk to the nearest drugstore, which was on a busy boulevard. Along the way, I guess he got something in his shoe and he bent down to get it out."

"Yeah? And?"

"Someone came speeding around a corner, lost control of the car, and ran into him. Turns out the guy was drunk. After he hit my father, he crashed through the front of a store window."

"Jesus."

"It crushed my father's right leg so badly, they had to amputate it."

"You're kidding me."

"No."

"All because you had the car?"

Alfie shrugged. "Some of the biggest things in life happen over the smallest turns in the day."

"OK, Socrates."

"It's true."

"And you didn't know about this until you got to the hospital?"

"They wouldn't tell me."

"And when you got there?"

"They took me to his room. He was asleep, on oxygen. His face was all bruised and purplish. His legs were covered by blankets.

"A doctor pulled me aside. He asked if my mother was around, or if I had any sisters or brothers. When I told him no, he said, 'In that case, you'll have to be his caregiver.' Once my father recovered, he said, he was going to need a lot of help, not just physically, but mentally. Getting used to missing a leg would be a big deal. He might feel depressed for a while. Even suicidal.

"When he said that, I felt sick. My father had been through many things in his life, but he was always ready to soldier on. I couldn't imagine him in despair. I stood over him as he lay in that hospital bed and kept thinking about the times he'd stared at my mother's photo. He'd already lost so much, you know? To be honest, I didn't think I could be much help if he were handicapped. I often felt more like a burden to him than a comfort."

LaPorta shook his head slowly. "I don't get it," he said.

"What?" Alfie asked.

"If you really have the power you say, why didn't you go back and redo the day?"

Alfie looked surprised.

"I did."

"You did?"

"Of course. I took one last look at him, then time jumped back to Saturday morning. We were having breakfast. Corn flakes and bananas. I remember being so happy to see him shoveling cereal into his mouth that he caught me staring and said 'What?' And I said 'Nothing, Dad.' And he said 'Stop gawking.' And I said 'OK, Dad.' But I was still smiling.

"Then he said, 'What time are you taking the car?' I thought about Gianna and the zoo and the day I was never going to have. And I said, 'I'm not going, Dad.'

"And I didn't."

LaPorta rubbed his chin.

"So that's why Gianna didn't remember anything."

"Exactly. And only after I jumped back in time did I realize I didn't have the phone number where she was staying. Just the address. There was no way to call to tell her I wasn't coming.

"Later that afternoon, after my dad had taken the car to buy his aspirin, Gianna called my house, kind of upset. 'Where are you?' she said. I told her I had car issues and didn't have her number. I was sorry. Could we do it on Sunday? But she said she was heading back to California. She hung up kind of quickly. And that was that."

"So the whole date," LaPorta said, "the zoo, all that stuff about you two connecting, it never happened?"

"It happened, but I'm the only one who knows it." Alfie paused. "Well. Now *you* do, too. And my boss, when she reads this."

LaPorta ran a hand across the table. "Man, oh, man," he sighed. "Your freaking existence."

"Yeah."

"*If* any of it is true."

"You still don't believe me?"

LaPorta shrugged. Deep down, he doubted Alfie was making up this *entire* thing. Too many details. Too many specifics. The story often made LaPorta think back on things *he* would have undone in his life. The football game his senior year where he destroyed his knee. That night with an attractive blackjack dealer that cost him his job at a New Orleans casino. How simple, if you knew the consequences, to avoid the dumb mistakes you make in life.

"It doesn't matter if I believe you," he said. "What matters is if you stole millions of dollars from a casino."

"So now it's 'if,'" Alfie said, grinning. "Good. We're making progress."

LaPorta glared at him.

"Shut up. Read."

THE COMPOSITION BOOK

Back at school, Gianna and I barely saw each other. She was pretty busy with classes and activities, and I didn't want to force things. I had to keep reminding myself that the affection we'd shared at the zoo was a nonevent to her. If anything, she was still angry at me for standing her up. That day felt like a secret only I was keeping. It sometimes got me in trouble.

"Can I ask you something?" I said once when we were sitting in the cafeteria.

"OK."

"Do you ever feel alone?"

She held a spoonful of yogurt halfway between the cup and her mouth.

"Why would you ask me that?"

"I don't know. Just wondering."

The truth was, I was using a confession that she made in another life to try and get closer to her in this one. It wasn't one of my finer moments.

"Why would I feel alone?" she snapped. "I have tons of friends. Do *you* ever feel alone, Alfie?"

"No," I lied.

She shook her head and swallowed her yogurt.

"You're pretty weird sometimes, you know that?" she said.

*

We went on this way for much of the year. I would help her study, or join her on a morning run, or carry boxes of flyers for the various causes she was involved in. But there was an invisible barrier that I could never cross, from the guy who carried her boxes to the guy who held her hand. Sometimes, sitting at a table with her friends, they would talk about potential boyfriends for her, and she'd say "Really? You think?" and they'd say "Oh, yeah, you should talk to him," taking no notice of the pained look on my face.

Elliot, my roommate from the theater program, kept encouraging me to broaden my social life. "Stop brooding over this Gianna," he'd say. "It's a huge school. Look at all the other women here!"

I wasn't really interested. But one night, after I'd spotted Gianna at a pizza place, laughing it up with a group of soccer players, I went to see Elliot perform in a show and afterward followed him to a cast party at a fraternity house. I got pretty drunk, still upset at the idea of Gianna with those guys. I was frustrated that our best memory wasn't a memory at all for her, and the special way she'd treated me that day at the zoo was something I might never experience again. Meanwhile, Elliot, who was wasted, had his arm around me and kept pushing me in front of his fellow cast members, yelling, "This is Alfie! He needs sex badly!"

One of those cast members was an exchange student from Ireland, a pretty girl with reddish hair, narrow shoulders, and a low-cut tank top under a flannel shirt that revealed a lot of cleavage. She said her name was Maisie, and when Elliot claimed I needed sex, she plucked at one of my shirt buttons and said, "Join the club, boyo."

I don't remember a lot of what happened next, except that there was a good deal more drinking and flirtatious pushing and grabbing and some grinding to music that had no beat. Then we were in somebody's room with a single desk light illuminating a Che Guevara poster above one bed and a Dallas Cowboys Cheerleaders poster over the other, and then Maisie and I were on a mattress and our clothes were coming off quickly, my shirt, her shirt, her tank top, my pants, and I felt the heat of her bare skin and her collarbone against mine, both of us grunting and fumbling down below and then a push and a softness and a groan from her and an exhale from me. I remember in the middle of it lifting my head to see Che Guevara, looking over us, and everything was spinning and —I know it sounds strange—but I saw the image of Gianna, her mouth agape, as if she couldn't believe what I was doing. As if to hide from her, I buried my head alongside Maisie's, her hair catching in my mouth. I heard the wooden bed frame squeaking beneath us and then it was over. I was panting like I'd been running up a mountain, and Maisie giggled between breaths and said, "Well, that was fast," and then she patted my naked back and added, "But fun." And again I lowered my head next to hers and she pressed her cheek against me and said, "Aww," as if touched by my tenderness. But it wasn't tenderness. I just didn't want her to see me crying.

*

So, if I haven't been clear about things, Boss, that was my first time. With a girl I'd just met, under the gaze of a Cuban revolutionary. I still don't know whose room it was. But the next afternoon, when I woke up in my dorm with a monster hangover, Elliot was reading at his desk, wearing big earmuff headphones. He grinned and yelled "He lives!" and then he said "How was Maisie?" and I mumbled "Yeah" and he yelled "What?" and I said "Fine" and he yelled "WHAT?" and I yelled "Take the stupid headphones off!" but he just nodded and said "Cool!" and went back to bopping his head and reading.

I felt like crap. Not just physically, but because that landmark moment had been with a near stranger, and not with the girl I'd truly desired. A better person might have gone to Gianna and told her that. Confessed his love. But that's not what happened.

Instead, over the next three weekends, I went to parties with Elliot and asked him to introduce me to any girls he thought might sleep with me. And he did. And they did. I don't have an excuse, any more than an alcoholic who falls off the wagon with one drink has an excuse for chugging down three more. Once I'd felt what sex was like, I wanted to do it again and, to be blunt, get better at it. And if we're measuring things by endurance, I suppose I did. By the fourth experience, I wasn't so astonished over everything I was touching and was able to stay with it longer.

After my most recent encounter, with a sophomore medical student named Danielle, I was walking back to my dorm room on Sunday morning, badly in need of a shower, when I suddenly heard Gianna's voice.

"Where are *you* coming from?"

I turned to see her lying on a bench, her head supported by a book bag, her camera pointed toward some trees. I shuddered like a caught criminal.

"Nowhere. Getting some breakfast."

She squinted. "Cafeteria's the other way."

"I know that," I said quickly. "What are you shooting?"

"Birds. They gather in this tree overnight. When the church bells ring at eight o'clock, they all fly away. I want to capture the moment they take off."

"Cool, yeah. What kind of birds?" I was stammering conversation. *What kind of birds? Really?*

"Chickadees," she said. "Maybe sparrows."

"Sparrows. Right. Yeah."

She put the camera to her eye.

"What's her last name?"

"Huh?"

"Whoever's room you're coming from. What's her last name?"

I swallowed. "What are you talking about?"

She pulled her head back from the camera and stared at me. A prison spotlight couldn't have made me feel more exposed.

"Guys never remember a girl's last name. You don't remember hers, do you?"

She held her gaze for a long, sad moment.

"Oh, Alfie," she said, putting her eye back behind the viewfinder. "You break my heart."

*

That conversation stayed with me for days, as things did anytime Gianna seemed disappointed in me. It's like that old song, if something is wrong with my baby, something is wrong with me. I score that as another entry in The Truth About True Love.

Later that week, I was in my room with Elliot, consumed by this funk, when I asked him, "Hey, do you remember that party where I met Maisie?"

"The one from Scotland?"

"Ireland."

"Right. Ireland."

"Was that a Friday or Saturday?"

"Friday, February third."

"Wow. You sure?"

"I remember 'cause it was Pete's birthday. Why?"

I didn't bother to answer. Instead, I whispered the word *twice* and landed back at that party, with a red plastic cup of beer in my hand. I looked at the crowd. I looked at the beer. I saw Maisie approaching and heard Elliot holler, "This is my friend Alfie! He needs sex badly!"

Before she could say anything, I yelled, "This is my friend, Elliot, he's totally wasted!" Then I lowered my voice to Maisie and said, "I don't really need sex."

"Too bad," she said.

I took an awkward sip of beer and excused myself. I went home a few minutes later. I didn't sleep with Maisie, or any of the other girls in the repeated weeks that followed. It didn't really change things. It didn't make me a virgin again. I was just trying to feel better about myself. And to be better for Gianna. Not that she knew anything about it.

*

Summer came, and once again, Gianna and I were three thousand miles apart. I called her in California, just to say hello, and she mentioned that she was coming to visit her roommate in early August.

"Can we please get together?" I asked. "I promise the car won't break down this time."

She half laughed and finally agreed. "But if you stand me up, Alfie, I will never speak to you again."

We arranged to meet on a Tuesday at noon. The plan was to walk around downtown Philadelphia, maybe get some pizza.

Two days before our rendezvous, they started talking about the weather. A huge storm was coming. A hurricane moving up the coast. I didn't want to know. I saw this day as a chance to clear the slate with Gianna, away from school, away from other friends or guys she knew. Nothing could interfere.

The night before, my father watched the TV news and said, "This storm is a whopper. They're saying we might get five inches of rain. Make sure you don't go anywhere."

"I won't," I lied.

Now, these days, Boss, I follow weather all the time, especially if it's going to be rough and I need to secure the beach house. Put up the storm shutters, check the caulking. It's part of my job. You even joke about me and rain, how I sit on the deck and stare at it, getting soaked. You once said "Alfie, you must be part frog." I guess it looks that way.

But back then, when I was twenty years old, wind, rain, lightning, they were just annoyances. If you wanted to do something fun, you found a way. And meeting Gianna was more than fun. It was going to be the day I told her how I felt.

*

I got to the city early. The air was thick, and the wind was already swaying traffic lights. You could feel the dark, looming clouds ready to explode.

Gianna and I had arranged to meet on the corner of Eighth and Market Streets, by a department store called Gimbels. I chose that spot deliberately, because her birthday was the following day, and I wanted to get her a present. A taxi dropped me off an hour before our meeting, and I went in and started wandering up and down the aisles.

There were few customers. I guess the storm had scared most people off. Searching for the right gift, I entered the women's clothing area and flipped through sweaters and blouses. Then I realized I had no clue what size Gianna was and would inevitably pick something wrong or insulting.

So I moved on to the perfume section, where a bored

worker offered to spray my wrist with fragrance. I realized I also knew nothing about perfumes. Or body sprays or eau de toilette, whatever that was. So I followed a sign into the jewelry section and perused the glass cases of rings, watches, necklaces, and bracelets.

"How much is that one?" I asked the saleswoman, pointing to a simple shiny stone on a gold chain.

"That's half a carat, bezel set," she said, pulling it out. "Very nice. It's two thousand."

She must have seen my Adam's apple jump up my neck.

"Maybe something simpler?" she said.

"Yeah," I rasped.

"What does she like? The person you're getting this for?"

I thought for a moment.

"Animals."

The woman smiled as if I were pathetic.

"The only things we have with animals are for children."

I nodded, as if that were obvious. Then I said, "Can I see those?"

Five minutes later, I had what I wanted. Or rather, what I could afford. Just then a voice came over the loudspeakers: *"Gimbels customers, we're sorry to announce that we will be closing in fifteen minutes due to the oncoming storm. Please make your final selections."*

A nervous energy spread through the place. Salespeople put away displays. The scant customers headed for the exits. I looked at my watch. Still twenty minutes before I was supposed to meet Gianna. I didn't want to get soaked before she got there, so I waited by the front, just inside the huge revolving doors, which kept spinning even when no one was going in or out. I guess they were on some kind of timer.

Outside, the rain had begun, and it was coming down in veils. The sky was occasionally shocked with lightning, and when the thunder burst, I could feel the rumbling even inside the store. *Of all the days*, I said to myself. I began to think Gianna showing up was a pipe dream.

I watched most of the employees leave through a side entrance by the customer service desk. Soon I was alone. I checked my watch again. Five minutes until our meeting time. The sidewalks were empty. Howling wind rattled the large windows.

I saw a bus splashing through the streets. It stopped on the corner. I whispered to myself, "Be on this bus. Be on this bus." And when it pulled away, as if someone up above had heard me, there was Gianna, wearing jeans and a yellow blouse and holding a handbag over her head against the downpour. My heart jumped. She darted toward the store and I tried to get her attention, but the rain kept her from looking up. I saw her shoot her gaze left and right, searching. When she finally looked straight ahead, I windmilled my arms, and she smiled at me. Even getting wet, handbag over her head, she smiled. It's something I would always love about her.

She jogged to the door, her sneakers splashing the pavement. I motioned for her to come in, because at least it was dry, but then I remembered they were closing and I didn't want us to get locked inside, so I jumped into the revolving door just as she pushed in to join me. As we circled each other we made the goofy "oops" face.

And then, at that very moment, all the lights inside Gimbels went dark and the revolving doors jammed in place, with me in one pocket and Gianna in another. She pushed. I pushed. They wouldn't budge.

"Alfie?" her muffled voice said. "What's happening?"

*

Our best choices often come when we have no choice. My mother used to say that. That day at Gimbels, Gianna and I tried pushing, slamming, even kicking at the doors that trapped us. Whatever had made them spin was now shut off. And with the store empty, yelling for help was fruitless. Eventually, Gianna plopped on the floor, and threw her hands over her knees.

Then she started laughing.

She shook her head and laughed some more so I laughed and then she laughed harder and we kept going until all the anxiety had been released. Finally, with her voice thinned by the glass, I heard her yell, "Oh, God, Alfie, why do I hang out with you?"

"Because I'm fun!"

"Yeah, right!"

"Come on! What could be better than this?"

"What could be better than *this*?"

"Yeah. What could be better than this?"

Outside, the rain was pummeling the sidewalk so hard it splashed back up like ricocheting bullets. The wind blew trash and newspapers up the streets. Lightning kept flashing, as if someone were messing with the world's electricity. And there we were, trapped inside the most unlikely of shelters.

"How long do you think it will last?" I yelled.

"What?" she yelled back.

"The storm!"

"What *about* it?"

"How long do you think . . ."

I stopped and shook my head. Didn't matter.

"Come closer!" she hollered as she shifted nearer the pane. I reluctantly did the same. I was always self-conscious about my face being too close to people. But Gianna, up close, was flawless. Not a blemish on her skin, her teeth perfectly spaced, her lips glossed with a shade of red lipstick that was seductive even through dirty glass.

"This reminds me of Africa," she said. "Remember when it would rain like this?"

I could hear her better now.

"Yeah," I said.

"It used to scare me," she said.

"Not me. I loved it."

"Really?"

"My mom used to take me outside and dance in it."

She laughed. "No way!"

"She was like that."

Her expression softened.

"Do you miss her?"

"She died a long time ago."

"But do you miss her?"

I hesitated. "Yeah. I still do."

Gianna smiled. "I met her once, you know."

I was stunned. "When?"

"She came with you to see Lallu. She was really sweet. She let me use this walking stick she had. I kept trying to pole vault with it. And when you guys left, she said I could keep it. She even hugged me. I still have that stick somewhere, I think."

I didn't remember any of this. But hearing it made me feel closer to Gianna than ever. Which loosened me up for what I said next. She was so near, yet beyond my reach, which is kind of how I'd felt about her for a long time.

"Listen, Gianna. Can I tell you something? As long as we're stuck here?"

"Sure."

I took a breath.

"I think about you a lot. Actually, all the time. It's weird. Being together as kids, even though we were so little, I feel like we're connected.

"I've felt this way for a long time. Ever since I saw you at the Miami zoo. To be honest, I came to college because of you."

Her eyes widened.

"I know that sounds creepy, right? I don't mean it that way. I just—I just wanted to be where you were. I like being around you. I know I've acted stupid sometimes—a lot of times. It's because . . . you make me nervous."

"Why would I make you nervous?" she asked.

"Come on. It's obvious, right?"

"What?"

I exhaled hard.

"That I like you. That I more than like you. I mean . . ." The words just spilled out. "That I love you. I really do. I know that sounds insane, we're not even dating or anything. I'm sorry. But it's how I feel."

My mouth went dry and my heart pounded. Suddenly, I felt like a complete idiot. *What are you doing? What were you thinking?*

"Alfie," Gianna said. "Do you mean all of this?"

"Yeah."

"Because you say a lot of weird things."

"No. Yes. I mean it!"

Then, as if she needed physical proof, I opened the bag and took out a small white box.

"Look. I got this for you."

I pulled off the top and removed a kid's necklace. Dangling from the bottom was a little silver elephant.

"For your birthday. Happy birthday, Gianna."

She blinked several times. It looked like she might cry. She put her hand to the glass and I pushed the elephant forward. She moved her fingertips as if touching it.

"Oh, God, Alfie," she said, smiling.

"What?"

"It took you long enough."

I exhaled so hard, I fogged up the glass. But when that moisture evaporated, she was staring at me with the most loving expression. And whatever man she was seeing that day was the man I wanted to be forever.

She curled her index finger. I moved my face closer.

"Nothing," she said.

"Nothing?"

"Nothing could be better than this."

She pushed her beautiful lips in my direction and I felt my nose brush the glass. That was our first kiss. Through a revolving door that a thousand dirty hands had pushed against that morning.

It was perfect.

NASSAU

"Well, hallelujah," LaPorta said, sneering. "You finally hooked the big fish."

He leaned in.

"How long before you got her in the sack?"

Alfie shook his head.

"That's all you're getting from this?"

LaPorta pushed back in his chair. "Am I supposed to be getting something else?"

Alfie cocked his head.

"Have you ever been in love, Detective?"

"Sure. Lots of times."

"I don't mean the lots-of-times kind. I mean the tumbling, can't-stop-thinking-about-her, can't-wait-to-see-her kind."

LaPorta smirked, but his mind did jump to his second wife, Barbara, and the summer they met in Las Vegas, a late-night swim they took after the pool was closed. They couldn't stop pawing one another in the water, bobbing and kissing and wrapping their legs around each other. Eventually, they ducked into a nearby cabana and yanked the curtain closed. He was still in solid shape in those days, stomach tight, chest firm, and he remembered the sensation of her body pressed against his, the dampness of their skin, her breath in his ear. He wanted every inch of her, every minute of her. It stayed that way for a while.

"Let's say I did," LaPorta offered. "What about it?"

"What Gianna and I had was like that," Alfie said. "Every day in college, I just wanted to know where she was. Every meal, we would sit together. If I went to a convenience store, I'd buy her a key chain or a little stuffed animal. Or she'd show up at my dorm room with a record album she'd bought because I said I liked a song on the radio.

"When I had exams, she left good luck notes under my door. If she got sick, I brought her chicken soup and nose spray. When we walked around, we held hands. When we watched a movie, she leaned her head on my shoulder. I couldn't be around her without physically connecting, you know?"

"Whatever," LaPorta snipped. He didn't want to let on that he'd experienced such feelings, too, but lost them along the way. He couldn't tell if Alfie's story was making him sympathetic or envious. It was definitely distracting, like getting caught up in a TV show when you're supposed to be doing work. He wanted to find out what happened with this Gianna.

But.

"What does *any* of this have to do with the two million dollars?" he asked.

"I told you, the notebook will explain everything."

"Or it won't, and you'll go to jail."

"I don't think so."

"Listen, pal. You gotta take this more seriously—"

His cell phone buzzed. He lifted it to his ear. "Yeah?"

"I have some new information, Vincent."

It was Sampson, his connection with the Bahamian national police. LaPorta rose and stepped into the hallway. He closed the door behind him.

"What is it?" he whispered.

"Your suspect went straight to the bank after the casino. He wired all the money out."

"I know that already."

"The big chunk went to that woman's bank account in Florida. Rule. Gianna Rule?"

"Yeah, I know—"

"But, listen. He went to another bank twenty minutes later. He did a second wire. Two hundred thousand. To Zimbabwe in Africa."

"*What?*" LaPorta grabbed his forehead. "Why didn't we know this before?"

"The teller who did the wire went home just before we got to the bank. We found him this afternoon when he came in for his shift."

"He confirmed?"

"Two hundred grand. To an account in Bulawayo, wherever that is."

"What kind of account?"

"It's a company. We're trying to find out who owns it, but it's the middle of the night there."

"Call me as soon as you get ahold of them."

He hung up and reentered the room. He studied Alfie, who was looking down and smiling at the page he had just read aloud. LaPorta admonished himself. He had actually started to root for this guy, hoping there was an innocent explanation for the whole roulette thing. But innocent people didn't wire money to foreign bank accounts and buy international plane tickets.

"Everything all right, Detective?" Alfie said.

"Just peachy."

"I know we're running short on time. So I'm going to skip ahead in the story, OK?"

LaPorta raised an eyebrow.

"What's your hurry?"

"Well. Aren't you anxious about Zimbabwe? The money I sent there?"

La Porta blinked. "What are you talking about?"

"Your phone call just now?"

"You heard that?"

"How could I hear it? You went out into the hall."

"Then how—"

"I figured you were going to find out sooner or later. Anyhow, doesn't matter, does it? We're on the same page here, Detective."

LaPorta dropped into his chair.

"Yeah? What frickin' page is that?"

Alfie flipped ahead in the notebook, then put both palms down on its corners.

"This one."

THE COMPOSITION BOOK

Not long after we got engaged, Gianna and I called my grandmother. We wanted her at our wedding. But the woman who answered the phone at the nursing home said Yaya wasn't doing well, so we—

NASSAU

"Wait a minute!"

Alfie looked up.

"You got engaged?" LaPorta said.

"Yes."

"You *married* this woman?"

"Eventually, yes."

"So she's your wife? Gianna Rule is your *wife*?"

"No," Alfie said. He looked down. "Not anymore."

"Whoa. You dumped her, and you're sending her two million dollars?"

"I didn't dump her."

"She dumped *you*, and you're sending her two million dollars? That's even worse!"

Alfie looked away.

"OK, now I gotta know," LaPorta said. "Go back."

"Go back?"

"I want to hear how you got her to marry you."

"You mean when I proposed?"

"Yeah. Read that."

"It wasn't a big deal."

"I'll be the judge."

"You sure?"

"Hurry up."

Alfie raised an eyebrow but, complying with the detective's request, flipped back a few pages, found a spot, and read from there.

THE COMPOSITION BOOK

After graduating from college, Gianna and I decided to move in together. The only question was where. Gianna was hoping to go to South America and pursue her dreams of photographing wildlife. But my passion was music. I wanted to try to make it in that business, which meant one place: New York City.

"We'll only stay a couple years," I said. "We can earn some money, and if things go right and I make good connections, then we can live wherever we want."

"Promise?" she said.

"Promise."

We pooled our funds, rented a studio apartment on the Upper West Side in Manhattan, and began a life of circling our dreams without ever realizing them. We took odd jobs to pay the rent. Gianna worked in a camera store. I got hired by a music public relations firm to write press releases, a skill I didn't even know I had. On weekends I gave piano lessons at a Brooklyn shop, and they let me rent an upright piano for cheap. Because our apartment was so small, we had to jam that piano between the kitchen door and our futon bed. We stacked record albums on top of it, and books on top of those. We kept our clothes in a trunk. We grew plants in the bathroom. The windows leaked in cold air during the winter, and because we lived in a single room, if one of us got sick, we both did.

There were times I was tempted to use my power for more money. Rent a bigger place. Buy a car. But my mother's warning about doing that stayed with me. And how would I explain to Gianna that we could suddenly afford such things?

Besides, there was something in our frugal existence that seemed to magnify our affection.

"Aren't you getting tired of me being this close?" Gianna once asked as she cuddled under the blankets while I dressed on the edge of the bed.

"Why would I get tired of someone I love?" I said.

She nudged me with her feet.

"That's the right answer," she said.

She pulled me down and pushed my shirt off my shoulders and we made love in the way we had blissfully gotten used to, tender, thrilling, satisfying. I could have stayed in those days forever.

*

Our building was pre–World War II, and we lived on the ninth floor, with an elevator that was often broken and a hallway that smelled of other people's cooking. On Sundays, we heard gospel music through the walls. There was an alley behind us with a faded green trash dumpster, and one day Gianna discovered some stray cats living there in a Dunkin' Donuts box. She brought them food every morning.

The months glided by. I wrote songs at night and tried to sell them to record companies or music publishers. For my twenty-fourth birthday, Gianna bought me a two-track tape recorder so I could make my own demos—she must have spent every dollar she had—and that night, we made instant hot chocolate and Gianna sat next to me on the piano stool. I pressed record on the new machine.

"What do you want to hear?" I said.

"Play that 'Try Me' song you always sang in college."

I placed my hands on the keys.

"Wait," she said, grabbing my fingers. "Can I ask you something?"

"OK."

"Did you ever do this with another woman? Sit and play for them? Like this?"

"No."

"Good. I want this to always be our thing."

She let go of my hand.

"What about you?" I countered. "Did you ever sit next to a guy who played a song for you?"

She thought for a moment. "Once. In college. With Mike. But he just banged on his electric guitar."

I looked down.

"Hey. Alfie?" Gianna said, turning my chin with her finger. "I was just waiting for you, OK?"

"What do you mean?"

"I mean, even in Africa, I sensed that you were somehow going to be in my life. When I saw you again at the zoo in Miami, I knew I was right."

"Then how come it took us so long to get together? In

college, you went out with other guys. You got mad at me a bunch of times."

"I told you," she said. "I was waiting."

"For what?"

"For you to grow up."

I didn't want to smile. But sometimes she made so much sense, I couldn't help it.

"Don't be hurt," she said, squeezing my arm. "Destiny is patient."

"You mean this was always going to happen?"

"Yup." She smiled. "If you went back in time it would all still happen again."

I think I visibly gulped. And then, feeling so close to her, I blurted it out: "I can do that."

"Do what?"

"Go back in time."

She grinned mischievously. "Oh, yeah?"

"I'm serious. I have a gift. I can do things twice. I've done it most of my life. If I don't like something the first time, I can travel back and try it again."

"I see." She narrowed her gaze, feigning seriousness. "And can you take me with you, professor?"

"What?"

"Can we go back in your time machine together, say, to Africa? And Lallu? Right now?"

I made a face. "It doesn't work like that."

"Ah."

"But what if it did?" I said. "What if you *could* go back and redo something? What would it be?"

She looked away. She breathed out softly.

"Nothing."

"Nothing?"

"It would be like taking a stitch out of a tapestry. The whole thing could unravel." She turned back to me. "I figure every little thing that happens is part of life or fate or God or whatever leading me to where I'm supposed to be."

She shrugged her shoulders. "Who am I to undo that? It's not finished yet."

I nodded blankly. I felt sheepish.

"So should I go back and erase this whole conversation?"

She took my arm. "Yes, please. I really don't want to think my boyfriend is insane."

"OK. *Twice.*"

I snapped back two minutes.

"Don't be hurt," she was saying, squeezing my arm. "Destiny is patient."

I looked straight into her eyes. "Yes, it is."

She pushed my fingers onto the keys.

"Play," she whispered.

I hit the first chord and sang the song she'd asked for.

> *"Try me, try me,*
> *Darling tell me, I need you*
> *Try me, try me,*
> *And our love will always be true."*

Gianna laid her head on my shoulder, and on the last verse she whisper-sang along with me. We kissed at the end and she said "That was really good, Alfie" and I looked around at our cramped apartment and this beautiful woman on my shoulder and the wisdom she had that I clearly did not and I swallowed hard and thought, *This is what they mean when they say "choked up,"* because I really was, choked up, and I pulled Gianna close and she threw her arms around my neck and I lifted her as she squealed with joy.

We made love on the futon, not bothering to open it. Afterward, lying next to her, I felt as full as I'd ever felt after my best meal, as rested as after my best sleep.

"I love our little apartment," Gianna whispered.

"Let's get married," I whispered back.

"Alfie," she said, cupping my face in her hands, "Alfie, Alfie . . ."

NASSAU

"That was it?"

Alfie stopped and looked up.

"Yes. That was it."

LaPorta stroked his chin.

"You're right. Wasn't much."

"Did it need to be?"

"Some people make a big deal. You know, hide a ring in the apple pie. That kind of thing."

"Is that how you did it?"

"Me? Nah." LaPorta chuckled. "My first wife orchestrated the whole event. Picked out the ring. Even picked out the box. Told me to give it to her at Christmas. Then she cried when she opened it. 'Oh, Vince, it's so beautiful!' I don't know. She liked to make a big production out of things."

"Is that why you split up?"

"Yes and no. She was a pain."

"And your second wife?"

"Well, that's a whole diff—"

LaPorta stopped himself. What was he doing? His story didn't matter. This notebook didn't matter. *Roulette scam. Two million dollars.* He glanced at his watch. The police would be here any minute to take Alfie to jail.

"Look, pal. I don't care what you read next. But if it doesn't explain why we're bothering with this notebook, you're done."

"It will," Alfie said.

THE COMPOSITION BOOK

We went to visit my grandmother not long after we got engaged. The nursing home was as I remembered it. But when Yaya was wheeled out, I was stunned at how much she had changed in a short time. She sat low in her chair, arms limp in her lap, her mouth slightly agape. Her beautiful hair, always full and youthful, was now matted back under a shower cap.

"Alfie," she said. "I didn't know . . . you were coming."

"I called a couple days ago. Remember?"

"Oh, you did? I don't . . . I'm . . ."

She looked down and shook her head. I nudged Gianna, who was standing behind me.

"Yaya, this is Gianna."

She lifted her eyebrows. "Oh. Gianna. Finally!"

She motioned for me to lean in.

"Let me jump back to this morning," she whispered. "I'll get cleaned up."

"No, Yaya. You're fine the way you are."

"You sure?"

"I'm sure."

She squeezed my hand, then raised her voice to Gianna.

"You are lovely," she said.

"Thank you," Gianna said. "Not as lovely as you."

"Oh, my, well," my grandmother said.

She turned to her orderly. "Go away," she snapped.

He rolled his eyes but headed down the hall.

"So, Gianna," my grandmother whispered, "you got any cigarettes?"

*

We visited for two hours. My grandmother drifted in and out. Sometimes she was right there, sharp as a needle, making comments about my haircut or how she hated answering machines. Then she'd nod off or repeat something she'd said five minutes earlier. She kept glancing at a small refrigerator, as if waiting for something to emerge from it.

But she and Gianna got along splendidly. Gianna had a warmth that touched anyone in her orbit. When Yaya drifted, Gianna held her hand until she was able to focus again. They spoke about Africa, college, photography, our apartment. She told Yaya how beautiful her skin was. At one point, still holding Gianna's hand, Yaya reached for mine. We edged our chairs closer together.

"This one," she said, nodding at me, "I worry about sometimes."

"It's all right," Gianna said. "I'll keep an eye on him."

"Promise?"

"Yes."

"I believe you." Yaya smiled deeply. "I want to give you something, OK?"

"OK..."

Yaya closed her eyes, still smiling. We sat that way for a few seconds. Then she opened her eyes and said, "Good."

"What was that, Yaya?" I asked.

"Just a little prayer."

"Thank you," Gianna said.

"So," Yaya said. "Will Alfie make an honest woman out of you?"

"An honest woman?"

"Marriage."

Gianna smiled. "Yes. He proposed."

"I don't see a ring."

"We're gonna get to that, Yaya," I said. "We're saving money."

"Is that yours?" Gianna asked, pointing to the jeweled band on my grandmother's finger.

"Uh-huh," she answered. She let go of our hands and ran her fingertips over the small stone. Her mouth curled downward.

"Go outside now, sweetheart," she said to Gianna.

*

Once Gianna had gone, my grandmother's tone changed.

"Bring me that," she said, pointing.

"The fridge?"

"The book on top."

I walked over. It was a photo album, open to the first page. I put it in her lap, and she ran her fingers over the faded images of an old black-and-white family portrait.

"My mother," she said. "And my grandmother. That's your uncle Nikos. And my daddy. Look how young."

I studied the familial faces, the men in suits and the women wearing embroidered Greek jackets, their hair tucked under tight-fitting hats.

Yaya flipped the page. "Now. You see that fellow?"

It was a fraying photo of Yaya at the beach as a young woman, standing next to a dark-haired man with a barrel chest and squat, muscular legs. He looked to be about her age.

"Who is he?"

"George. From the Seminole reservation. That's the only picture I have of him."

"A friend?"

She shook her head wistfully. "More."

"More?"

"He loved me a lot."

I chuckled. "Well, not more than Grandpa."

"More than anyone," she corrected. "He wanted to marry me."

"How did you feel about him?"

She closed the book. She covered her eyes.

"What's the matter, Yaya?"

Her chin dropped. I thought maybe she'd fallen asleep.

"Alfie!" she suddenly said, her eyes springing open. "You have to know this!"

"What, Yaya?"

"Love is different. If you change your mind, if you jump back and start seeing someone else, your first love will never love you again."

"What are you—"

"It's the only thing you can't do twice!"

"I don't understand."

She tapped the photo several times.

"George. We got *involved*, you see? It was wonderful. True love. But my parents wouldn't allow it because he was different. So, I went back. I undid things. I started seeing your grandfather. I gave my love to him. But it wasn't the same. It didn't feel as strong. So one night, I snuck out to see George again."

"And what happened?"

Tears filled her eyes.

"It was gone. The way he felt. The way he looked at me. I was just another person to him. I tried so many times. So many jumps. It never worked. What we'd had was erased."

I handed her a tissue. She wiped her cheeks.

"This woman. Gianna. Is it true love?"

"I think it is."

"Then I'm worried, Alfie."

"About what?"

"That you'll do something stupid."

"Yaya!"

"Like I did!"

"Yaya. What do you think I'm going to do?"

She waved her fingers dismissively. We sat in silence. I heard the sound of someone vacuuming the hallway.

"I'm sorry, Alfie. I'm old. This is what being old is. You worry about the young."

I didn't know what to say. She looked so frail.

"Yaya?"

"Mmm?"

"Why don't you go back a few years? Just to be healthier?"

"Oh, Alfie, I already have. So many times."

She gripped the photo album. "At some point, you get tired of reliving the past. You're ready for what comes next."

The finality in her words frightened me.

"I don't want to lose you, Yaya."

She looked at me tenderly.

"I want, and you want, and God does what God wants."

"That's what Mom told me."

"Well." She smiled. "Who do you think told her?"

NASSAU

Alfie paused his reading. He leaned back.

"She died a month later."

"Was she telling the truth?"

"About what?"

"That you can't get someone to love you twice?"

"Yes."

"And was she right about you? That you were bound to make a mistake?"

"I've made many."

LaPorta chuckled. "You know, for people who get to do things over and over, you folks have a lot of regrets."

"That's true." Alfie's eyes narrowed. "Maybe because the second time, you can't blame anyone but yourself."

"Whatever."

LaPorta's phone buzzed. He read the screen.

"Looks like we're done here, Alfie Logan."

"What do you mean?"

"I mean you're going with the police now."

"But we haven't finished the story."

LaPorta rose from his chair. "I'm going to hear another story."

"What are you talking about?"

He flipped his phone around to show a text.

"We've located Gianna Rule. And—what a coincidence—she's staying on the island."

"Wait. She's here?"

"This oughta be interesting," LaPorta said, grinning.

As the detective opened the door and yelled for the guard, Alfie's expression changed. He creased a page in the notebook and carefully closed it around his fingers.

Four

THE COMPOSITION BOOK

A lot of couples fight over their wedding plans. Gianna and I never got the chance.

Her parents had moved to Abu Dhabi, so finding a date when they could attend was tricky. And whenever we discussed venues, Gianna would say, "I'm happy with anything," but when I'd suggest a place, she'd scrunch her face and say, "Oh, not *that*."

So we left it open, being in no rush, until one Saturday after a particularly disappointing week. Gianna had submitted photos to a magazine, pictures of birds in various New York City locations—outside a Macy's window, or sitting on a pretzel vendor's cart. I thought they were really good. But the magazine rejected them as "too cliché." Meanwhile, I had finally gotten an appointment with a record company executive but arrived late for our meeting because the subway broke down. They told me he'd gone into another meeting and I should try to reschedule. Instead, I *twiced* myself back to an earlier train, arrived on time, and figured I'd avoided the worst of it.

But once we sat down and started playing my cassette, the executive's phone rang and he spent the next three minutes in conversation. He hung up as the last notes of my best song ended and said, "Sorry, man, I just don't hear it." There was no going back on that.

So Gianna and I were both pretty fed up, and on Saturday morning she said, "Let's drive as far away as we can get in a day." We rented a car and headed west through the Holland Tunnel, out into New Jersey and on through Pennsylvania, trading frustrations over the people who had rejected us, until the landscape changed and we rolled down the windows and we stopped talking and put some music on the radio. The sky brightened, and eventually we smelled pine needles. We saw a sign that said ALLEGHENY NATIONAL FOREST.

"Let's get out and walk," I said.

We hiked for an hour without a map or a destination, shedding the city's weight with every muddy step. Eventually we came upon a small town near the Clarion River. I don't even remember what it was called. But there was a general store, and we went in to buy something to drink.

A small bell clanged when the door opened. Behind the counter was a tall Black man wearing a tweed cap. He looked to be in his sixties, with a well-trimmed graying beard. We were the only customers, and he smiled broadly at us.

"Here from New York?" he said. His voice was heavily accented.

"How do you know that?" I asked.

"Well, let me see." He hooked his fingers together. "You seem weary, as if you have not slept. And you opened the door harshly and entered in a hurry."

Gianna and I glanced at each other. Had we really become such ugly creatures of the city?

"Also," the man added, pointing to my chest, "there is that."

I looked at my T-shirt, which read MANHATTAN BOXING CLUB. The man burst out laughing.

"I am many things," he bellowed, "but not a mind reader!"

We laughed along. Then Gianna asked, "What other things?" She was always picking up on people's sentences that way.

Within minutes, we learned the man's name was Dozie, that he'd emigrated from Nigeria in his twenties and had worked in this general store until the original owner, an elderly woman, passed away and, to his surprise, left him the business in her estate. That was twelve years ago, he said. In a town as small as this, he'd had to learn to wear many hats. Volunteer firefighter. Election official. Tree trimmer.

"Why did you leave Nigeria?" Gianna asked.

"Silly me. I fell for an American woman and married her. She used to work here beside me." He paused. "She passed last year."

"I'm sorry," Gianna said.

"I am sorry, too. It's a wonderful thing, to be married to an excellent person."

Gianna glanced at me. I could tell she was happy we'd taken this trip.

"May I ask, are you two . . . ?"

"Engaged," Gianna said. She made an exaggerated frown. "Still waiting on a ring."

"Ah, well, we can take care of that," Dozie said.

He pointed to half a dozen toy rings in a foam rubber display. Gianna plucked one out and put it on her pinkie finger. She held it up, admiring the cheap sparkle.

"Now, if only you were a justice of the peace."

Dozie grinned. "As a matter of fact..."

We looked at each other.

"You're joking," I said.

"I am not. I have officiated more than thirty weddings in our town."

Gianna grabbed my hand. I felt a nervous flush.

"Alfie," she said, "do you want to get married today?"

There were a million things I could have said at that moment. A witty retort. A mushy concurrence. A simple yes.

But what I said was: "*Twice*."

*

Instantly, I was back in the car that morning, driving through the Holland Tunnel. Gianna was complaining about her magazine editor. I mumbled "Yeah" and "You're right." But inside, my heart was racing. I thought about not stopping at that forest. Never going for that walk.

Yet as we rolled through New Jersey and into Pennsylvania, I realized there was no good reason to wait. I loved Gianna. She loved me. Nobody came close to making me feel as happy, as understood, or as appreciated as she did. Perhaps living life recklessly the first time—knowing I could always erase things later—hadn't prepared me for a moment of real commitment. I'd panicked. I felt ashamed.

Just then Gianna, for no reason, reached across, took my hand, and without a word, pulled it into her lap as she gazed out the window.

"Hi, honey," I whispered.

She turned and smiled. "Hi, honey."

With that, something inside me melted. And for the first time in all the years of my magical undoings, I left everything as it was, because another truth in The Truth About True Love is that when it's good, you don't want to alter it. The walk through the woods. The encounter with Dozie. I left every detail untouched, right up to the moment when Gianna asked, "Alfie, do you want to get married today?"

This time I smiled.

"I do," I said.

Dozie threw his hands in the air. "Wonderful! We only need a few things . . ."

He moved quickly to the shelves, pulling off several items.

"Cayenne pepper," he said, grabbing a shaker, "for the passion, yes? A lemon, for life's disappointments. Some vinegar, for the challenges you will face.

"And this . . ." He grabbed a jar of honey. "For the sweetness and joy."

He placed the goods on the counter. "If you taste these four elements during your ceremony, it means you will understand what lies ahead in marriage."

"That's beautiful," Gianna said. "Did you make that up?"

"Yes. Well. First, I saw it done in Nigeria. *Then* I made it up!"

We all laughed. And that is how it happened. In a ceremony officiated by a Nigerian-born general store owner and witnessed by a mail sorter from the post office next door, Gianna and I recited unrehearsed vows. We tasted those four elements. When Dozie asked if we trusted each other in all things, we said we did.

"Good," he said. "Suspicion and belief cannot share the same bed."

When he finished, I got down on one knee and sang a chorus of "Try Me" to Gianna. Then I placed the toy ring on her finger. We were officially wed, against a backdrop of chirping birds and a gurgling river. And I wouldn't dream of changing a moment.

Until I had to.

NASSAU

LaPorta hurried through the hotel pool area, past palm trees planted in neatly spaced concrete squares, and rows of open white beach chairs. Sampson, the Bahamian police officer, matched his stride. They ducked in through a side entrance to the casino, moved briskly past the craps tables and the endless rows of slot machines, and turned down a corridor to the security office.

Although LaPorta was curious to speak with Gianna Rule, he had stopped at the casino first, because a witness had unexpectedly come forward. A blackjack dealer. He was waiting in the hallway, alongside a security guard.

"In here," LaPorta said, motioning toward the door.

The dealer was thin, with a stringy mustache. When they sat him down, he began chewing on his fingernails. LaPorta flanked him on one side, Sampson on the other.

"You have something to tell us?"

"Yes."

"Talk."

His voice was taut with nerves. He said his name was Toussaint. He'd come to the Bahamas from Haiti.

"Two weeks ago, this man who live in my apartment building knock on my door. He ask if I know a roulette croupier here. I say yes, I know one very good. We come from Haiti together. The man ask if he can be trusted and I say, sure, I trust him with anything."

"And then?" LaPorta said.

"Then he ask if I want to make some money."

"What did you say?"

"I say sure. I like money. But I need my job, I cannot get in trouble, or maybe they send me back to Haiti. He say not to worry, all I have to do is introduce my friend to the American."

"What American? What was his name?"

"I never know his name."

"What did he look like?"

"Tall. He have an earring."

Alfie, LaPorta thought. *I knew it.*

"When did they meet?"

"Last week."

"What did they talk about?"

"I don't know. I leave the room. I don't want to get in trouble. But . . ."

"But what?"

"When my friend come out, he is hiding something in his hand."

"Did you see what it was?"

"A ball."

"What kind of ball?"

Toussaint shrugged as if it were obvious.

"A roulette ball," he said.

*

Twenty minutes later, the dealer was on his way to police headquarters while LaPorta and Sampson drove to The

Ocean Club Resort, where Gianna Rule was registered as a guest. The downtown traffic was thick with jitneys and rental cars. LaPorta, riding in the passenger seat, stared at the sherbet-colored buildings dotting the crowded streets. He remembered when he first arrived in the Bahamas, being told the color scheme was intentional. *Pink is government, yellow is schools, and green is for police.*

He lowered a window and inhaled the humid air. A clearer picture was beginning to form. Alfie had recruited a croupier. The phony ball was rigged. At a prearranged time, the croupier slipped it into the roulette wheel, and Alfie knew when to put his money down.

There were likely others involved, too. These schemes usually required a lookout, a person to distract security, maybe additional bettors to make the illegal move less obvious. LaPorta had requested video of the roulette table from an hour before Alfie sat down. The faces of everyone who even momentarily stopped there would be run through their system. If anyone else helped pull off this swindle, it would be caught on tape.

Still, one thought nagged at the detective. How did Alfie know exactly which number to play? A rigged ball might fall heavily to one side of the wheel, but to an individual number? That would require some truly advanced level of technology.

"Hey, Vincent?" Sampson said, interrupting his thought.
"Yeah?"
"This woman we're going to see. Who is she?"

"The suspect's wife. Ex-wife, actually."

"What does she have to do with it?"

"Well, he sent her the money. We need to find out if she—"

Sampson slammed his horn at a jitney that had cut in front of him.

"Look at this fool!"

LaPorta blew out air and shifted in his seat. In his briefcase was Alfie's notebook. At the right moment, he planned to reveal it to Gianna Rule, but not until she tried to deny her part, or maybe even knowing Alfie. That was usually how it went. *I never heard of the guy. I don't know what you're talking about.*

Deep down he was curious about meeting this Gianna, seeing if she matched Alfie's glowing description, and what it was about her that was so captivating. He thought about his own wife. He took out his phone and dialed her number in Miami.

"Hey, Vince," she said, answering.

"How's it going?"

"OK. I'm seeing my mom this afternoon."

"Uh-huh."

"And you? Chasing any bad guys?"

"One."

"What'd he do?"

"Cheated on roulette. Stole two million."

Even as LaPorta said the words, he realized he was trying to impress her.

"Wow."

"Yeah."

"Just be careful, Vince. You're not a real cop, remember."

And there it was. The stinging comment he could always count on.

"Yeah, Barbara. You keep reminding me."

"Am I wrong?"

"No, Barbara."

"Are you carrying a gun?"

"No, Barbara."

"I'm just saying."

"Fine."

"I'm looking out for you, Vince. So you don't get hurt."

"I don't need you to look out for me."

"Right. Because you're not a cop."

"OK. Good talk."

"Look, I'm not trying to—"

"It's fine. Gotta go. Gotta do some not-a-cop business."

He caught Sampson looking at him. His wife wasn't wrong. He wasn't technically a law enforcement officer. And Bahamian law forbade private gun ownership.

But the bigger truth was that his relationship with Barbara, a second marriage for both of them, was a series of combustible confrontations like these, followed by apologies, then a period of calm, then confrontations again. It was one reason she stayed in Miami when he took this job. They saw each other as often as his work would allow, and for now that seemed satisfactory.

LaPorta hadn't really thought about the meagerness of

"satisfactory" until Alfie and all his true love talk. It made him reflect on the choices in his own love life and their hollow results. Working in the islands, LaPorta often saw couples arm in arm, spontaneously kissing or groping one another—on the beach, on the street, in the restaurants. It made him envious. He'd had that once with Barbara. At the beginning, they couldn't keep their hands off each other. But years passed. They started arguing over money and how much time she spent with her mother. Everything cooled. What was it they said about passion and rocket fuel? They both burn fast?

A tourist bus pulled alongside the police car, and the smell of diesel was pungent. LaPorta rolled up the window and adjusted the air-conditioning. Then he reached into his briefcase and took out Alfie's notebook. He tilted it on its side and noticed something odd. A single page had been folded back. It was fairly near the end, which felt like more than a coincidence.

What are you up to, Alfie?

LaPorta flipped to that page and began to read.

THE COMPOSITION BOOK

Things my mother said she loved about me:

9. *"Your shyness when you meet new people."*

Now, Boss, comes the part that you might find hardest to believe.

I became, briefly, famous.

It happened in the 1990s. By this point, Gianna and I had been married for twelve years. We were in our thirties, and as I've mentioned in the previous pages, our relationship had shifted toward practical matters. Coordinating work schedules. Saving money to buy a house. And discussing having children, something Gianna yearned for.

Sadly, I did not. My music career had never taken off, but the press release job revealed a talent for writing that I didn't know I had. I spent all my time on that now, mostly freelance stories for magazines and newspapers. Music had been so subjective; I could never tell why someone didn't like a song. But with writing, my gift for jumping time proved invaluable. I could turn something in, find out what the editors didn't like, then go back a few days, redo it, and give them exactly what they wanted. It got me a reputation as someone who could get big stories done well quickly. Which got me paid more.

It also meant I could get assignments at any time and have

to suddenly go away for a stretch, then bury myself in trying to meet a deadline. I didn't see how raising a baby would fit with that. And if I'm being truly honest, I bristled at sharing Gianna's attention. I liked the fuss she made over me. Little notes she'd leave around the apartment. Having my favorite albums playing when I got home. I knew she would embrace motherhood and worried her focus on me would diminish. That's a selfish view, one I am ashamed to share. But selfishness is always clearer when you're looking back on it.

There was also this concern: how would my power work with a child? If I traveled back to before the baby was born, would that baby be the same? And having lost people I loved, my mother, Wesley, Yaya, did I want to become so deeply attached to another soul whose final fate, despite my gift, I could not alter? I convinced myself it was better not to take such risks.

This, as you might imagine, created friction with Gianna. "Come on, sweetie," she would whisper in bed, "don't you want to make a mini me-and-you?" Other times, when I voiced hesitations, she'd snap, "Alfie, you have no idea what it's like to feel your fertility withering!"

I was tempted to undo those disagreements, go back, erase them from Gianna's memory. But if I did, I would still remember them. Which would make us uneven. And uneven in love is unhealthy.

So I left those arguments alone. I took the smooth and the rough with Gianna, because it was us. Part of the tapestry, as she had once said.

Still, our marriage *was* shifting, as most do over time. We'd moved to a bigger apartment. We'd traded coziness for workspace. The romantic meals we had cooked together were now more often Chinese takeout. We went to bed at different hours, wearing sweats and T-shirts.

Gianna took these changes in stride, and I tried to do the same. But I did miss the spontaneity. The passion. Sometimes, when she was sleeping, I would stare at Gianna's face and remember the aroused way she made me feel when we were younger, arriving at her door and imagining us in bed before the night was done. What is it about time and love that turns us from red with desire to pale with familiarity?

*

The famous part of my life also coincided with my becoming, momentarily, rich. Yes, Boss. I once had a lot of money. You might find that strange, seeing as I've been living in small apartments or your guest house all these years, and rarely wearing anything fancier than khakis. But remember, this is a story of my lives before this life, and of so many things that were different.

I want to say that money was never an issue with Gianna. She was decidedly nonmaterialistic, often warning how finances change relationships. And my mother, as I've said, had warned me never to use my second tries for wealth.

But, I admit, I did try once, in our first year of marriage. Gianna's birthday was coming up and she was still wearing that toy ring from our wedding. I wanted to get her a real one. Something impressive.

I had read about a computer stock that had soared in price over its first three days on the New York exchange. Figuring even my mother would be on board with a ring for my wife, I *twiced* myself back a week and found a broker to invest five hundred dollars the day the computer stock debuted. It quadrupled to two thousand before I sold it. I went to a jewelry store on Forty-Seventh Street and spent all the money on a small, round-cut diamond in a bezel setting.

On her birthday, I took Gianna to an Italian restaurant, and after the food came, I said I had something special to give her. She opened the box and her eyes bugged out. "Oh my God, Alfie, it's so beautiful." She put it on and kissed me. She flipped her hand left and right. I was happy.

"But, Alfie, how can we afford this?"

I didn't really have a plausible lie, so I made the mistake of telling her about my stock success.

"You don't follow the stock market," she said.

"I had a hunch."

"About a computer company?"

"Someone at the magazine suggested it," I said, lying.

She stared at me, then poked her pasta with a fork.

"What's wrong?" I asked.

"It's luck money," she said.

"What's 'luck money'?"

"The kind you don't earn. It doesn't feel right."

I exhaled. "Can't you just enjoy it?"

Her expression changed. She took my hand. "I'm sorry, Alfie. This is really sweet. You strike it rich—and you think of me. I do love you for that."

We kissed, but I felt so bad that I time jumped back an hour and kept the ring in my pocket. We had a great night anyhow. And I learned another Truth About True Love: it doesn't have to cost you anything.

Even when it might cost you everything.

*

So now. To what made me famous.

I was sent to Mexico by *Life* magazine to do a story about a distance runner who was deaf due to a birth defect. The young man, named Jaimie, was supremely gifted; at age eighteen he had already set a world record in the 1500 meters. He was hoping to compete in the Atlanta Olympics later that year. His family lived in a small village. His father had died, and Jaimie worked as a dishwasher in his mother's restaurant. Her name was Marisol, only thirty-five herself, but older-looking from the endless hours she spent in the restaurant kitchen. The small profits she made went to pay for her son's training.

We used a sign language translator for our interviews. Jaimie was a sweet kid with a sharp sense of humor. At one point he lent me a pair of his running shoes, and we did a few laps together around a track, with me desperately trying to keep up. When we finished, he signed to his translator, "Ask him when I can take the chains off my legs."

I stayed for a few days. The morning I was scheduled to leave, Jaimie, Marisol, the photographer, and I were heading to the restaurant when we stopped at a bank to make a deposit. It was a small branch, with one teller and a couple of desks. The door was open to the heat.

Jaimie signed to his mother that he would fill out the deposit slip while the photographer took Marisol across the way to get some shots. A minute later, three men in sweat suits entered the bank. I watched two of them move quickly to the teller. The third lingered by the door. I turned my attention back to Marisol and the photographer.

Suddenly, I heard a gunshot. I spun and saw the man by the door holding a pistol in the air. He started screaming in Spanish and everyone inside—Marisol, the photographer, the workers, the other customers, and me—all dropped to the ground.

All except Jaimie.

His back was turned so he couldn't see what was going on, and obviously, being deaf, he couldn't hear the commotion. The gunman shouted at him and drew closer, waving his pistol. But Jaimie had his head lowered, writing. He never saw the guy until he snatched away the deposit envelope. Jaimie instinctively lunged for it, and the gunman shot him twice in the thigh.

Marisol screamed. Jaimie crumpled to the floor. The three robbers raced out the door. Suddenly the place was silent, save for the agonizing cries of a young athlete holding his bleeding leg and likely wondering if his future had just been erased.

I panicked. I'd never seen anyone shot before. I slammed my eyes shut and shouted *"Twice!"* But the image in my head was of us entering the bank. Instantly, we were there again, Jaimie heading to fill out the deposit slip, Marisol and the photographer moving to the window.

I froze. I hadn't gone back far enough. Before I could even yell anything, the three men walked in, and two of them again headed to the teller. My head swiveled from them to Marisol to the guy at the door.

BANG! The gunman fired and yelled at Jaimie, and the only thing I could think to do was run for him. If I could get him to the ground, maybe the gunman would leave him alone. I sprinted Jaimie's way and saw him glance up just as I dove for his legs, tackling him like a linebacker. I heard the gun fire and the teller screaming and I felt Jaimie beneath me and a hot sting in my shoulder. The three robbers raced out the door and I fell off Jaimie and glanced down to a mess of blood around my collarbone.

"Alfie!" the photographer yelled. "Oh my God, you're shot!"

I shut my eyes and whispered *"Twice-twice-twice!"* but nothing happened—I'd redone the moment already—and as I clamped my jaw against this newfound pain, I realized that whatever followed, this was one mistake I was going to have to live with.

*

The bullet, thank God, went straight through. I spent a week in a Mexico City hospital before they let me go home. Gianna was waiting at the airport. She burst into tears when she saw my arm in a sling.

"Oh, no, no, no, Alfie—"

"It's OK," I said as she threw her arms around me. "Could be worse."

"You got shot. How could it be worse?"

There were a million answers to that. But I said nothing. Gianna tended to me during the weeks that followed in a gentle, loving way that showed itself in all the small things—my coffee waiting in the morning, an extra pillow for my shoulder, a bottle of ibuprofen on my nightstand, a second washcloth prepared after cleaning my wound with the first one.

I must admit, I wasn't the best patient. Not because of the injury, but because *Life* wanted the whole story, and quickly, and typing one-handed was pretty difficult. Meanwhile, other people were interviewing Jaimie, who credited me with saving his life. When he made the Olympic team in Atlanta, he announced as a tribute he would race in the shoes that he'd lent me.

He won his event by more than two seconds, again setting a new world record. I was there to witness it. At his press conference, he asked me up onstage.

"Without Mr. Alfie Logan," he signed, "I would never

have this." He held up his gold medal and put his arm around my neck. Cameras whirred and flashes popped.

As you might imagine, the story took off. Suddenly I was getting calls from TV shows to do interviews with Jaimie and Marisol. We appeared on several programs, and the crowds were enthusiastic. It didn't hurt that Jaimie had a great smile, while his mother, who did the signing for him, was humble and funny. I let them tell the tale of the bank robbery. They made me sound braver than I was.

One day, after the three of us did a morning talk show in New York, I returned home to find two voicemails on my answering machine, both from movie executives in California interested in buying the *Life* magazine story for a film. I listened to their messages with Gianna.

"What do you think?" I asked.

"I think you told the story already."

"But not as a movie."

"It *wasn't* a movie."

That silenced me. Gianna had a talent for saying one thing that dammed up a conversation faster than a cork in a bottle.

*

In hindsight, I wish I'd left it there. But I didn't. I was intrigued by the idea of a film. I knew a literary agent from my magazine work, and I asked him to get involved. He made some calls, talking up the story. The next thing I knew, I was flying to Los Angeles to meet with multiple interested parties, which my agent said was the best possible scenario.

"Just tell the tale as dramatically as you can," he instructed, "and before you leave let them know you're meeting with other people. I'll do the rest."

And so, to rooms full of fascinated faces, I told the story again and again during four studio meetings. The first three were largely the same. An airy office and a sizable conference table. Bottles of Perrier. Young executives cooing about the drama of the robbery while tossing around names of famous actors who could play the various parts.

Just before the last meeting, in a huge conference room on a high floor of a Hollywood talent agency, I asked if I could use the phone to call Gianna. She sounded frustrated when she answered.

"What's the matter?" I asked.

"The shutter broke on my camera. I just had it fixed last year. Now I have to take it in again."

"We should buy a new camera."

"I don't need a new camera. I just need a shutter that works."

"Sorry."

"I was hoping to go to the Bronx Zoo tomorrow."

"Again?"

"Yes, again. Why?"

"Nothing."

The zoo was all she had left of her photography dreams. She often went there when I was out of town.

"Well, I hope you can fix it," I said.

"I will. Sorry. I'm just frustrated. How are your meetings going?"

"Good, I think. They seem interested."

"When are you coming home?"

Just then the door swung open and four people entered. Three of them looked like the other executives I had met, young men in jeans, baseball caps, shirts untucked, but the fourth was a woman you would have noticed from another zip code. I knew her face from the movies, but when you see such a familiar face in the flesh, you blink, as if something about it can't be real. Her hair was blond as wheat, her eyes shielded by amber sunglasses, her skin perfectly tanned, her teeth almost impossibly white. But it was the command with which she moved that captivated me. I wondered: Do stars become stars because of a quality the rest of us don't have, or is it learned? Either way, she took my breath.

"Alfie . . . ?" I heard Gianna say again. "When are you coming home?"

"Let me call you back. We're gonna start."

I hung up before she finished her "OK" as the woman approached and extended her hand.

"Hi, I'm Nicolette Pink," she said.

"I know," I mumbled back.

*

Now, I'll spare you all the business details that followed, Boss. Suffice it to say a bidding war ensued, as my agent had predicted, and we had multiple offers to make the movie for a crazy price, but ultimately chose the studio that had Nicolette Pink as its partner, because she wanted to direct the film and star in it as Marisol. She was, at the time, maybe the biggest actress in the country, the winner of several major awards, although her most popular film was a raunchy comedy in which she played an oversexed high school teacher.

We signed the papers and they sent me a sizable check—and another to Jaimie and Marisol in Mexico. They hired a big-name screenwriter who wrote a script that only loosely followed the real story. He took numerous liberties, including this one: instead of me being married, in the movie I was single and ended up falling in love with Marisol (played by Nicolette, with her blond hair colored a sable shade). The explanation was that the film "needed a love story." I had no say in this—you give away such rights when you take the money—and was completely surprised when I read it.

But not as surprised as Gianna.

"What is this?" she asked, holding out the script like a smelly fish.

"What?"

"You're single? You fall in love with Jaimie's mother?"

"I know." I sighed. "It's just a movie."

"So they make things up?"

"I guess."

"Doesn't Jaimie think it's stupid? Or Marisol?"

"They probably don't care."

"They're using your real name."

"I know."

"And theirs."

"Because it's based on a true story."

"But this—" She held up the script. "Is *not* a true story."

"What do you want me to do, Gianna?"

She shook her head. "You already did what I didn't want you to do. Why ask me now?"

She tossed the script on the couch.

"You don't want to finish it?" I asked.

"Why should I? Like you said, it's a movie. I'll watch it when it comes out." She looked away. "Or I won't."

"Hey, I'm sorry," I said, leaning down and touching her knees. "It's out of my hands."

I saw she was crying.

"It's wrong," she rasped. "You falling in love with someone else."

"I know."

"Can't you give the money back? Tell them no thanks?"

"They gave money to Jaimie and Marisol, too, remember? They need it."

She exhaled and looked away. For a while she said nothing.

"What?" I whispered. "Gianna. Talk to me."

"I want to have a baby."

I swallowed.

"All right."

"All right?" she repeated.

Her face changed. Her eyes lifted. Her smile lit me up. I'd do anything for that smile. Even something I didn't mean.

Which is what I had just done.

*

Now, at this point, Boss, you're likely saying "I don't remember a film with Nicolette Pink where she played a runner's mother and fell in love with a journalist." There's a reason for that, which I will detail. But I need to explain something bigger first. Something that changed my life with Gianna forever.

The movie was being shot in Mexico, and I spent a lot of time on the set, at Nicolette's request. Because Jaimie was in training, and Marisol was running her restaurant, I was the only one available to verify certain details, especially with the actor playing me. Nicolette encouraged that. She was highly focused and professional during the shoot. But at night, when she invited me to view the edits of the day's filming, she often let her guard down. We spoke candidly. She was honest and quick-witted.

One late session, she shared stories about her life as an actress, the lewd advances she had to tolerate from producers and directors when she was coming up, and their constant emphasis on her looks, weight, and skin.

"I wouldn't think you'd have to worry about that," I said.

"You'd be surprised," she replied. "This"—she waved a hand at herself—"takes a lot of work. And you're never not 'on' in this business."

"Why did you go into it?"

She sighed. "I don't know. I had a lousy childhood. I came to California on my own when I was still a teenager. I was running away from who I was, the stuff I'd gone through. Acting, getting to pretend you're someone else, seemed like a good way of dealing with all that, I guess. Like you're getting a second chance, you know?"

"Yeah, I know," I said, trying to ignore the irony.

She smiled and leaned back. Her tapered white shirt clung to her thin waist.

"There was a movie once named *Alfie*," she said. "Did you ever see it?"

"No. But my mother nicknamed me for it. Well. For that song."

"No way."

"Yeah."

"Alfie was a ladies' man, you know."

"That's what I've heard."

"*What's it all about, Alfie?*" she warbled, singing the first line from that song, the way everybody does. Then she reached for the hair behind my left ear. "Ooh . . . you've got a real cowlick sticking out here."

"Sorry," I said. I felt a jolt though my body when she touched me.

"Why are you sorry?" She pressed it down gently. "It's not a flaw."

"Right. Yeah. Sorry. I mean. You know."

She turned back to the screen, then slumped, as if it were homework.

"My eyes are blurry," she said. "Do you want to get a drink?"

NASSAU

"Jesus," LaPorta mumbled.

"What are you reading?" Sampson said.

"The suspect's notebook. It's all garbage, I think."

"Why do you say that?"

"You know that actress Nicolette Pink?"

"From the high school teacher movie?"

"Yeah. He says she made a movie about *him*."

"What was it called?"

LaPorta flipped through pages. "I don't even know. It was about a Mexican robbery and a writer who gets shot."

Sampson shrugged. "Never saw it."

"Me neither."

LaPorta undid his safety belt, which was digging into his shoulder. He studied the gnarled traffic.

"How much longer?"

"If I cut behind the bus depot up ahead, I can swing around south of the beach and get to the hotel that way. Maybe ten minutes."

"Do it."

As Sampson eased the car over, LaPorta reached for his cell phone and called the police officer who was taking Alfie to jail.

"Hello, sir?" the officer answered.

"Everything good?"

"Yes, sir."

"Suspect with you?"

"He's in the back . . . Wait . . ."

LaPorta heard muffled conversation.

"He says he wants to talk to you."

LaPorta squeezed his fingers between his eyes. "All right. Put him on."

A long pause. Then.

"Vincent?"

"You call me Detective."

"Detective. Are you still reading?"

LaPorta sighed. "I'm stuck in traffic, so as a matter of fact, I am."

"Where I marked?"

"You mean the bent page?"

"You found it?"

"Very clever. What difference does it make?"

"All the difference, if you finish."

"I'm a little busy, Alf—"

"If you want to make sense with Gianna, you'll need to finish."

"OK, lover boy, thanks for the tip."

Sampson glanced over. LaPorta made a face, as if to say *This guy is nuts.*

"Why don't you concentrate on confessing, Alfie? Let me worry about your ex-wife."

"She won't understand," Alfie said.

"Oh, I'll be very clear. Especially about the two million."

"She'll say she doesn't know what you're talking about."

"That won't surprise me."
A pause. "Something else will."
"Yeah? What's that?"
"Keep reading, Vincent."
He hung up.

THE COMPOSITION BOOK

My father died nine years ago, Boss. Remember when we were working in Morocco and I asked for some time off? I actually went home to Philadelphia. I never told you, because I didn't want you feeling sorry for me. You didn't know my dad. Not in this life, anyhow. There was an earlier time when you met him. Spoke to him. Even laughed with him. But I had to undo those moments, and you'll have no recollection of them. Revealing this might make you rack your brain. Spare yourself. When I wipe a slate, I wipe it clean.

Dad died from a stroke, or the complications of one. He was with his second wife, Monica, in a New Jersey supermarket, when his legs buckled and he thudded to the floor. The stroke made his left hand involuntarily lock around the shopping cart handle, so his limp body was hanging on with one arm, like a lost sailor grasping a buoy at sea.

By the time they got him stabilized at the hospital, he couldn't move his appendages, his speech was slurred, and his eyesight was nearly gone. Monica called me in Morocco and told me the doctor said the next twenty-four hours were critical. I couldn't take a chance on getting home too late.

So I time jumped back eight days and flew to my old hometown and the house where I grew up. And I spent what turned out to be the final week of my father's life sleeping in my childhood bedroom, taking him out for breakfast every morning, playing a few rounds of golf, and having a final conversation that I'd long wanted to have.

*

"You feel like getting a root beer, Dad?"

"Yeah. Why not?"

We had just finished eighteen holes and were passing an old drive-in fast-food joint named Burt's. It had been there forever. We ordered through the window: two root beers and four hot dogs. Then I parked in the back, away from the other cars, and with the doors open and the sun beating down, we shoved the doughy rolls into our mouths and sipped noisily on the sodas through straws. Off in the distance someone was mowing grass.

"We haven't done *this* in a long time," my father said.

"Not since I was a kid."

"You know, once you retire, you have more leisure time than you thought you would." He paused. "It's nice of you to take a week off, Alfie. Nice to have you around."

"Thanks."

I watched him cradle the hot dog. His hands shook slightly. It had been two years since I'd seen him; he'd aged considerably. His close-cropped hair was white above his eyeglass temples, and the whiskers on his jowls caught the light like sprinkled salt.

"Dad?"

"Hmm?"

He took a long, slow bite.

"Can I ask you something? It's about Mom."

He nodded.

"Did she ever talk about having a different life? Before she got, you know, religious?"

He glanced at me but said nothing. He swallowed, wiped some mustard off his lips, then cleared his throat.

"Why are you asking me that?"

"Because just before she died, that day in Africa, she told me that she'd changed."

"Changed?"

"Yeah. She said she'd been a different type of person before, a selfish person who lost her heart and soul. I never remember her that way . . . Do you know what she was talking about?"

I studied his reaction. I wanted to see if my mother had ever told him about her power, to know if we shared that secret. It felt important. I'm not sure why. When you realize you are about to lose a parent, you suddenly want to know everything, say everything, share every little detail you omitted during the years when you were taking them for granted.

"Your mother suffered, Alfie," my father said.

"Suffered from what?"

"An illness." He paused. "A mental illness."

I blinked. "What are you talking about?"

"She imagined things. She was haunted by events that never happened."

"Like what?"

He crumpled a napkin in his fingers and turned his gaze out the open car door. "Like she'd been a drinker, for one."

"A drinker?"

"Yes. An alcoholic. So bad she'd gone to jail."

"Mom went to jail?"

"That's what she imagined."

"I never saw her drink."

"She did when we first met. But then she suddenly stopped. She never had a problem. And God knows she never went to jail." His voice lowered. "Or met up with other men. Or left the country..."

"Wait. She told you she did all that?"

"No. I found out after she died."

"How?"

He looked back at me. "Her therapist."

"Mom had a therapist?"

"For years, apparently. When we came back from Africa, the woman got in touch with me, you know, to say she was sorry. She said that Mom had been a brave woman over the years. She was surprised I never knew about their sessions.

"I asked to meet with her. I begged her to share what Mom had said. She refused at first, because of the ethics, you know? But I said our time together was so short and now that I wouldn't get any more, I wanted to know everything I could about her."

He paused. "That's when she told me those stories."

I was stunned.

"What did you say, Dad?"

"I said they had to be lies. But apparently, your mom had shared all these details about the years after you were born. She'd said she'd suffered postpartum depression, that she'd become a terrible alcoholic, that I'd come to visit her in jail, and you had, too, and she felt really badly about that. She'd even run away from us for a stretch.

"I didn't know what to tell this therapist, except that whoever Mom was talking about wasn't the woman I was married to."

He shook his head for several seconds, as if stuck staring at something that didn't make sense. "It was crazy, Alfie."

I took a deep breath. "I'm sorry, Dad."

"I guess it's only right that you know."

"Thank you."

"It's OK."

"But, Dad?"

He looked up.

"I need to tell *you* something."

"All right."

I put a hand on his shoulder. He glanced curiously at the gesture.

"Mom wasn't lying. She had a gift. She was able to do things twice in her life. She could go back in time, redo events. All that stuff? It probably did happen, and then she undid it, which is why we don't remember. You and I only remember the second version."

My father snorted, then half smiled. "Are you trying to make me feel better with this silliness?"

"No," I said. "I'm trying to tell you the truth. Because I guess she never could. She really did have that power."

I paused. "And I have it, too."

"To go back in time?"

"Yes."

My father looked away. He started rocking back and forth nervously.

"Alfie," he said softly, "are you OK? Your health?"

I squeezed his shoulder.

"I'm OK."

"I think . . . maybe I didn't do a very good job bringing you up."

"That's not true, Dad. You did great. You did everything you could. Why would you say that?"

"Because . . ."

"What?"

"Because you're not well. You're becoming delusional. Like she was."

I dropped my head. Why had I told him? I felt like a cave dweller who finally ventures out into a blizzard, only to realize he was better off in the cave.

"Dad. Listen." I lowered my voice. "I want to say how much I love you. And if anyone didn't do a good job, it was me. I didn't appreciate all you had to go through. I'm sorry. For everything."

His eyes were tearing up.

"I don't understand," he said shakily. "What's happening here?"

I forced a smile. "Nothing that will matter."

I pulled him close. His cheek rubbed against mine.

"*Twice*," I whispered.

Instantly, we were back at the golf course parking lot, getting into the car. I turned the ignition and flipped on the radio. A few minutes later, we were cruising past Burt's.

"Remember that old place?" my father said, pointing.

"Yeah. They served root beer."

"And terrible hot dogs."

"Yeah. Awful hot dogs."

My hands gripped the steering wheel.

"You played good today, Alfie," my father said.

"You did, too."

"For an old man, you mean?"

"Yeah. For an old man."

He chuckled. I was so grateful for his smile, I nearly cried.

*

I tell you that story, Boss, because it was the last time I redid anything in my life—until yesterday. And yesterday couldn't be helped. I'd been staying away from my gift deliberately, kind of like an addict who swears off his poison. Life has been different in the present tense, I'll admit that. You pay closer attention to things. You're more appreciative. More accepting.

But it wasn't losing my father that led to this decision.

It was another woman.

NASSAU

"Well, OK," LaPorta mumbled, thumbing the page. "We're finally talking about yesterday."

"What's that?" Sampson said.

"This story."

"I thought you said it was garbage."

"It is, I guess. I don't know. I think I'm getting to the part where he confesses."

"Well, do you want to read or do you want to do your job?"

"What do you mean?"

Sampson killed the engine.

"We're here."

LaPorta looked up. He had been so engrossed in the notebook, he didn't realize they were in the parking lot of The Ocean Club Resort. He stared through the windshield at the blanched-almond facade, and the guests lounging on their balconies. He was torn. The notebook might help him solve the case. But Gianna Rule was a suspect, given the money she was sent. And every passing minute was a minute when she could slip away.

"Ahhrrg," he groaned, pushing his palms against his forehead. Then he dog-eared the page he was reading and shoved the notebook into his bag.

"Let's go," he said.

Five

THE COMPOSITION BOOK

Things my mother said she loved about me:

10. *"The way you always tell the truth in the end."*

So back to Nicolette Pink. You probably think you know where I'm going with her, Boss. What actually happened was more complicated.

That night in the editing studio was a Friday, and we weren't shooting anything the next day, so Nicolette and I went back to the hotel and she asked me to join her at the bar downstairs. I stopped in my room to change and found an overnight mail envelope under my door. It was from Gianna. I didn't open it.

When I got downstairs, Nicolette had changed, too, into a gray corset top and a short black skirt. We sat near the back and she called over a waiter. She insisted I drink with her.

"Nobody likes a watcher," she said, grinning.

We stayed there for a couple of hours, drinking and talking the whole time. She told me about growing up in a trailer in rural Oklahoma; I told her about living in Africa. She told me about her parents splitting up when she was twelve; I told her about Adeline hiding my mother's photograph in a closet.

There was a piano player in the corner and a crowd that shrank as the night went on. Several times, we were interrupted by people who wanted Nicolette's autograph, which she always obliged, apologizing to me afterward. I was surprised at how polite she was to me. I guess I thought movie stars only wanted to talk about themselves. But she was considerate, and laughed heartily whenever I made a joke.

We traded sips as we continued our conversation, and I found myself studying how her mouth met the glass, the deep red of her painted lips pressing on the clear rounded edge. I warned myself to knock it off, to stop thinking about how attractive I found her.

"Can I ask you something?" she said.

"Sure."

"That day in the bank. What made you run to save Jaimie?"

I hooked my hands together.

"I'm not sure. It happened so fast."

"Were you afraid you might get shot?"

"I guess. I mean, I hoped I *wouldn't* get shot."

She chuckled.

"What?" I said.

"You're being modest. Most people don't 'hope' they won't get shot, then run in front of a gunman to save somebody."

She placed her fingers on top of mine.

"I admire that," she said.

I froze.

"Honestly?" she added. "It's . . . kind of a turn-on."

"Oh yeah?" I mumbled, because those were the only words that came to mind.

"Oh yeah," she said playfully, tapping her fingers lightly

on mine. Then she pulled away, lifted her glass, and gulped the rest of her drink. I caught myself glancing at the hollow of her neck. Her slim fingers. Trying to change the subject, I asked if she'd ever been married. I knew she hadn't. I asked anyhow.

"No," she said, looking away. "I mostly meet actors, and it's not a good idea to put two acting careers under one roof. I know couples like that. It doesn't work. They say they aren't competing, but..."

She waved a hand at the waiter and pointed to her glass.

"...they are. It ruins things, you know?"

She dropped her cheek into her palm and gazed across at me. "Writers are different. I wish I could write. I envy you, working alone, nobody directing you. It's great, right?"

"Um, yeah, sure," I stammered.

As the piano player was finishing "Night and Day" he hit a bad chord, and I mumbled, "Ooh, that wasn't good," probably because her looking at me made me nervous. Then Nicolette said "What wasn't good?" and I said "That chord" and she said "The piano player?" and I said "Yeah" and she said "Why? Do you play?" and I said "I used to."

A minute later, the pianist rose and left for the night. The place was emptying out.

"Go play something, Alfie," Nicolette said.

"Oh, no."

"Please? I'd love to hear you. Come on."

I hesitated, then rose, thinking *OK, maybe it's best to leave the temptation of this conversation.* But Nicolette followed me to the piano, carrying her drink, and to my surprise, she slid in next to me. Her hip pressed against mine and our shoulders touched. I diverted my eyes from her breasts, which were all but spilling out of her top when she leaned forward.

"Um . . ." I said.

"Um?"

"What do you want to hear?"

"I don't know." She smiled as if sleepy. "Something happy."

Something happy. For some reason, all I could think of was that old Jimmy Durante song "Make Someone Happy" from *Sleepless in Seattle,* I guess because it had the word *happy* in it. I started playing.

"Oooh, I love this one," Nicolette said. "Can you sing it, Alfie?"

So I sang. It's an easy, cute song. When I got to the part about "fame, if you win it, comes and goes in a minute," she slipped her arm through mine. Then she sang along on the final lines. She knew it word for word.

> *"Love is the answer,*
> *Someone to love is the answer,*
> *Once you've found her*
> *Build your world around her,*
> *Make someone happy,*
> *Make just one someone happy*
> *And you will be happy, too."*

When I finished, Nicolette stared at me.

"Alfie Logan, you are full of surprises."

Her arm was still hooked in mine, and she lowered her head onto my shoulder. I instantly flashed on the image of Gianna in our first apartment, and how, sitting at the piano, she asked if I had ever done this with anyone else. It flooded me with guilt.

"We should go, huh?" I croaked.

"All right," she whispered.

Nicolette rose, rubbing against me, her skirt rising as we made contact before falling gently back onto her thigh. I'm embarrassed to say how excited I was by this woman. Two minutes later we were at the elevator and Nicolette was swaying, humming that song to herself.

"Make . . . someone happy . . . Make one person happy . . ."

When we got in, we pressed our respective floors—hers was the penthouse, I was on eighteen—and she reached out and intercepted my hand and placed it firmly on her hip. She pressed against me, kissed me hard, and grabbed my belt and began to undo it.

"Lemme see, lemme see," she murmured.

I was dizzy from the drinks, dizzy from the idea, and so aroused that for a moment my muscles tightened and I couldn't move, I just let her do what she was doing. But there are planks that we walk and planks we jump off, and finally, at the sound of my zipper, I stepped back off that plank and said, "I can't, Nicolette, I'm married. You know?"

She pressed her eyes closed and spun away as if dancing.

"Right" she said, and then, "Right . . . right, right," kind of singsongy-drunk, and then the elevator pinged and the doors opened and I could all but touch the freedom in the air of the eighteenth floor. I backed out fast and blurted, "Thanks-a-lot-see-you-OK." As the doors closed, she was straightening her skirt and not even looking at me.

I staggered to my room as if walking through a wind tunnel. I let myself in. I saw the envelope from Gianna on the bed. I opened it. It was a Valentine's Day card, with a photo of the two of us inside. I hadn't even remembered it was Valentine's Day. I put it down and called our apartment.

Gianna's voice was groggy with sleep.

"Alfie?" she mumbled. "What time is it?"

"Time to come home," I said.

NASSAU

Gianna Rule, dressed in a bra and shorts after a shower, spread her various camera lenses across the hotel bed. She'd already been out yesterday on a day-long shoot and was planning a few more hours this afternoon. The sea life in the Bahamas was incredible, and she'd photographed some creatures she had never seen before. Rock iguanas, for one. They were an endangered species and the reason she was here, a magazine story on proposed oil drilling that threatened the island's marine life. The hope was that the beauty of her photographs would inspire opposition.

"Time, time, time," she mumbled, searching for her phone. She lifted a dirty T-shirt and a paperback book, then finally found it under a pillow.

"Ahh, no," she moaned. It was nearly two o'clock. The car was supposed to meet her in five minutes. She called her assistant but got no answer. She pulled on her sandals.

Suddenly, her room phone rang, and the shrill noise startled her. She stared at it, thinking about the news she'd gotten yesterday, that her ex-husband was here on the island. Her assistant had seen him wandering around the lobby. At first, she wondered if he was stalking her again. He'd never liked the way things ended.

But maybe it was just a coincidence. There was a big new casino here, drawing lots of tourists, and her ex had become enamored with gambling over the years. Either way, if this was him calling, she wanted no part of it. She let the phone ring until it stopped.

She hurried to the mirror, slapped on some moisturizer and a little makeup, then tousled her hair. She was proud, maybe a bit surprised, that at her age, she didn't have much gray. It helped her look young, which, much as she hated to admit it, also helped her in the photography business. She yanked on a long-sleeved cotton hoodie to protect her from the sun, then grabbed three lenses and shoved them in her camera bag. She did her typical spin around the room, making sure she wasn't forgetting anything.

As she pulled the door shut behind her, the room phone started ringing again.

THE COMPOSITION BOOK

It's obvious by now, Boss, that I've hidden many things from you. I am sorry. Secrecy is a loan against your better judgment. You pay the interest in regret.

I have kept my illness under wraps. This will make you mad, and perhaps sad. But please don't feel sorry for me. I knew this was coming. For what it's worth, I know how my life will end. I'm already having trouble walking. Next, I'll have a stroke. I'll lose my ability to speak. After that, I'll need to be fed and bathed. And soon my brain will stop communicating with my lungs. When they fail, so will I.

That stroke is coming soon. I've suffered it once. I will suffer it again. Despite my remarkable power, I'll die like anyone else, having done what I could with what I had.

So, please, keep reading. And let me correct the biggest mistake of my life.

*

The six months after I returned from California were, for Gianna and me, like a second honeymoon. We had money from the film option, so I didn't take any new assignments, and I encouraged Gianna to cut her work schedule at the camera store. For the first time in a long while, we had unhurried hours together. We took weekend trips. We stayed up late watching movies. We brought food to the alley cats in the morning and ate breakfasts in half-empty diners after most people had gone to work. We visited the Bronx Zoo many times, Gianna bouncing along, snapping photos while I carried her equipment over my shoulder.

We made love often during that stretch. The first night after I returned, I'd been so attentive to her body that afterward Gianna purred, "You should go to California more often." I smiled at her, but deep down I knew my focus—that night, and for much of the time that followed—was forged in guilt, perhaps the world's strongest motivator for man's temporary good behavior.

When thoughts about Nicolette Pink arose, I suppressed them. Nothing really happened with her, or at least what did happen, I had resisted. That's what I told myself. And what you tell yourself long enough becomes, like new paint on an old wall, the only color you see.

*

The movie finished filming and was scheduled to be released in late November. We received an invitation to a premiere in Los Angeles. It came in a large, expensive-looking envelope and had red felt lining and embossed lettering.

"Do you want to go?" I asked Gianna.

"Not really. But you do, right?"

I did and I didn't. My ego surely wanted to see this story on a fifty-foot-high screen. But the idea of my wife and Nicolette in the same place was worrisome. I hadn't seen her since that night. After that elevator encounter, I didn't know how I'd start a conversation.

In the end, Gianna made it easy. She had scheduled her annual doctor's checkup long before we knew about the premiere. It fell on the day before, and rescheduling would have pushed it out another two months.

"You go," she told me. "Have fun."

"All right."

My stomach clenched. *Have fun?* What is it about guilt that shades even the simplest phrase?

I got my hair cut. I purchased a new blazer and a fashionable shirt. When the time came, I boarded a plane at JFK and flew six hours to the West Coast.

When I disembarked at the Los Angeles airport, I found a pay phone and called Gianna.

"I'm here," I said.

"Alfie?"

Her voice sounded odd.

"You all right?"

"I went to the doctor today."

"Everything OK?"

"Yes."

"Good."

"Alfie?"

"Yeah?"

"Alfie?"

"What is it?"

A beat.

"We're pregnant."

NASSAU

LaPorta banged down the house phone. If Gianna Rule wasn't in her room, she could be anywhere. Maybe leaving the country.

"Should we check outside?" Sampson said. "The pool?"

"I don't know what she looks like."

"No picture?"

"No."

LaPorta thought about Alfie's description in the notebook. A stunning woman with dark hair. A woman whose smile could knock you over. Someone like that might stand out. Then again, it was just a suspect's words. For all LaPorta knew, Gianna Rule was as plain as cardboard.

The elevator door opened and three people exited. LaPorta glanced, then glanced back quickly, because one of them was an attractive dark-haired woman with a shoulder bag, and protruding from it was the rounded top of a camera lens.

Alfie. The zoo. Gianna taking his picture...

"Excuse me," LaPorta yelled, louder than he intended. Several people turned but not the woman, who kept walking.

"Excuse me!" he repeated, stepping toward her. "Gianna Rule?"

She stopped. "Who are you?"

"Are you Gianna Rule?"

She stared for a moment.

"I'm sorry, I need to be somewhere," she said, moving past.

LaPorta nodded to Sampson, who stepped in front of her, flashing his badge.

"You're gonna be late," LaPorta said.

THE COMPOSITION BOOK

A single thought can change every part of you. How you walk, how you smile, how you listen, how you breathe. I did go to that premiere in Los Angeles, but I felt like I was going in costume. The whole time I was shaking hands or blinking against flashbulbs, I was thinking, *I am going to be a father.* The idea turned every sound into background noise. It was a new sensation. It was also terrifying.

Looking back, Boss, I think it scared me in part because of the unusual life I had gotten used to—double time, double chances. I didn't know how I would use my gift once a baby came, or even if I should. I also realized I might eventually pass my strange power on to this child, as my mother had passed her power on to me.

All this was going on in my head—while I was about to be portrayed on a giant movie screen.

And then Nicolette arrived.

She was dressed in a silver lamé gown, backless, low-cut in front. Her ample hair—dark in the movie—was once again a blinding blond. There were hundreds of people trying to talk to her, but when she saw me, she hurried over. She took my hand, formally, but held it longer than one usually does, and gently rubbed her thumb across my palm.

"Hi," she said.

"Hi, Nicolette."

"I've missed you. Are you good?"

"Yeah. And you?"

"Everything's great."

I couldn't tell if she meant with life or with us. She was so calm. Meanwhile, my scalp was sweating. I think it must have showed, because she leaned in and lowered her voice.

"It's OK," she said. "Let's go make someone happy."

I forced a grin, because I couldn't come up with words.

"I'll see you after?" she said.

"Yeah," I said.

She was yanked away as cameras flashed.

And that was it.

I never did see Nicolette afterward. I went straight to the airport and caught a red-eye flight home, as I'd promised Gianna I would do.

When I walked through our door, just after 7:00 a.m., I was still dressed from the premiere, wrinkled, grimy, my lower back aching from trying to sleep on the plane. The light was dim and the apartment was silent. I stood there, knowing Gianna was in the bedroom, waiting with our big news, and I hate to admit this, Boss, but I didn't move. I couldn't get the image of Nicolette out of my mind. Undressing me in the elevator. Rubbing her fingers in my hand. Was it guilt—or something worse? A desire to be there rather than here? I slammed my eyes shut and shook my head to clear it.

"Alfie? Is that you?"

And there she was, my now-pregnant wife, leaning against the bedroom doorway. She wore a Boston University T-shirt and white sweat pants, her hair matted from sleep, and she smiled when she saw me as she always did. But quickly, that smile drooped.

"What's wrong?"
"What do you mean?"
"You look funny."
"I'm just tired. You know those flights."
"You sure?"
"Yeah."
She took a big breath.
"So . . ."
She opened her palms.
"Ready to be a daddy?"
I went to her quickly and squeezed her body against mine. But I never answered the question.

*

Now, I want to explain the next six months, Boss, because I've never spoken about them to anyone. I'm not sure I realized their significance until recently. Some events in life you process as they happen. Others take a lifetime to understand.

Gianna loved being pregnant. She followed all the health tips. She stopped drinking alcohol. She even halted certain physical activities like roller skating—which we used to do in the park—just to be safe. She insisted we look for a bigger apartment.

"But I like where we live," I protested.
"It's not just you and me anymore, Alfie."

I accompanied her to the obstetrician and picked up prenatal vitamins at the drugstore. I chased down foods for her cravings. But the more excited she got planning for the baby, the more outside those plans I felt. I grew short-tempered over little things, and we fell into petty arguments, most of which I traveled back and undid, because I didn't want her remembering this time as combative. I must have said *twice* at least three times a day.

Gianna could sense I was struggling. She constantly reassured me, rubbing my arm as she lay in my lap, whispering, "Alfie, it's going to be great. It really is. You'll be an amazing father."

I went along, taking deep breaths and hoping the idea would embrace me. Then, one afternoon, early in Gianna's fourth month, I came home from playing basketball with friends. She was sitting by the window, her hands on her belly.

"I just saw Sam," I said. "There's a Brazilian festival by the river tonight. He and Annie want us to go with them."

"No thanks, Alfie," she said, smiling.

"Why not?"

"No reason. Just taking it easy with the baby."

I frowned. "The baby's not due for five months. We're allowed to go out."

"It's Friday. It'll be crowded."

"So? That's the fun of it. There'll be music, food."

"I just don't want to."

"What if *I* want to?"

I said it more sharply than intended. I thought about jumping back a few minutes, but this had become a recurrent issue; part of me wanted to hash it out.

"Is this going to be us now?" I continued. "We don't go anywhere? We don't do anything fun? We just sit around thinking about a baby?"

Gianna didn't say anything. She looked hurt.

"I'm sorry," I mumbled, "but, you know . . ."

"It's OK," she said, rising. "Let's go. We can have fun. You're right. It's not against the rules."

We met our friends a few hours later. Sam and Annie were our age, not married, still in that pawing-each-other-at-every-moment stage. They brought beers over as soon as we arrived and banged them on the table.

"Let's celebrate the end of a crappy week," Sam said. "I worked my butt off."

"Thanks, but I can't drink," Gianna said.

"Oh, right, sorry," Annie said.

"No, no, don't be sorry, you all go ahead."

"You sure?" I said.

"Yes. It's fine."

So I drank with our friends. It felt good to be out. The festival had loud, energetic bands, and Sam and Annie danced the samba. Gianna said she was too tired, so we remained at the table, silently watching our friends wiggle and laugh. Finally, I got up to explore the row of food booths. I returned with large plates of barbecued beef, fried cod, and cheese bread.

"Oh, yes! Thank you!" Sam said, plopping down, sweaty from the dance floor. "I'm starving."

"Me too," said Annie.

We began gobbling it up, but Gianna left her plate alone.

"Eat something," I said.

"I'm not really hungry."

I slumped. "Really? Are you just gonna sit?"

Sam and Annie glanced at each other. They could see I had embarrassed my wife.

"It *is* delicious," Annie offered.

Gianna nodded reluctantly and lopped some beef on her bread. She tried the fish as well. We made small talk for another hour, and Sam and Annie ordered more beers. Eventually, we caught a cab and headed home.

"Admit it," I said, sitting next to her. "It was good to get out, right?"

She sighed. "I guess so. I'm sorry I'm so dull lately, Alfie."

"And I'm sorry if I'm impatient."

She smiled. "Well. You *are* impatient."

"But you . . ." I took her hand. "Are never dull."

We kissed gently, which should have been the end of that episode.

It wasn't.

In the middle of the night, Gianna began throwing up.

"You OK?" I mumbled when she came back to bed.

"I thought I was done with morning sickness," she said.

She groaned through the next few hours. I felt her forehead, which was hot. She said she had a migraine.

By sunrise, I was feeling it, too. I was sweaty and ran to the bathroom several times.

"I bet it was that food," I said, emerging from the toilet. Gianna lay in bed with a cold rag on her head.

"My stomach really hurts," she whined.

"Mine, too," I said.

I later learned we both had food poisoning. But our consequences weren't equal. Gianna's abdominal pain grew worse. By evening, it was so bad, I insisted she go to the hospital. In the emergency room, she threw up again, and the first doctor who saw her, a young Vietnamese physician, immediately sought out a senior staffer. An older doctor came in, checked Gianna over, then said a few words which I didn't understand.

Suddenly everyone was moving quickly and Gianna was being wheeled into an operating room, because the baby, they informed us, had no heartbeat.

*

I will spare you the details of the miscarriage, Boss, except to say we entered the hospital as expectant parents and we left as something else, unexpectant, if that's a word, not just of a child but, in time, of a certain happiness. We seemed to cross into a new, barren country, a gray place where dreams were mostly lost causes.

In the days that followed, Gianna was in shock. In the weeks that followed, she was in mourning. As the weeks turned to months, and she read about how food poisoning can sometimes lead to miscarriage, she got mad. And I became the target of her anger.

"Why did we go to that stupid festival? Why *did you make me go?*"

"I didn't make you go!"

"You did! I told you I wanted to stay home! If I'd have stayed home..."

She didn't finish. She just cried. And every subsequent time she brought this up, I was stung by the grief of unchangeable circumstances, which is not a feeling I'd known very often. My mother's death. Wesley. And Yaya. Other than those, pretty much anything that hurt me in life, I had changed. Now, suddenly, with the worst thing that had ever happened between Gianna and me, I was powerless.

Did I think about jumping back to avoid that festival? Of course. But I knew the rules. Our baby had died, which meant no matter what I did, I couldn't save it. It was going to happen, that day, that time, even if Gianna and I had sat inside a room with the doors locked. I couldn't watch my wife go through that again.

I wanted to tell her this. To let her know that I would have used whatever power I had to undo things, but this was beyond both of us.

I couldn't get this across without telling her everything. And it wouldn't have changed the pain of it. A heaviness fell over our kitchen table, our couch, our bed. We drifted into resentment. When it came time to try again, at first I didn't want to. Then she pulled away. Months later, when we both agreed to make the effort, our lovemaking felt more clinical than romantic.

Gianna did get pregnant eventually, twenty months after the first go-around. But she lost the baby again, this time after nine weeks. It happened in the middle of the night. I heard her crying in the bathroom. I got up, but the door was locked.

"Don't come in here, Alfie," she sobbed.

And sadly—despite how deep our love had been—that sentence became a theme. *Don't come in here.* We locked each other out of our hearts. We spoke. We ate. We slept in the same bed. But a connection had been severed.

A few months later I came home from work and she was silently grilling two lamb chops. No music. No "Hi, Alfie." Just the dull sizzle from the frying pan. I looked at her in her sweatshirt and pajama bottoms and said, "I'm going to make a sandwich."

"What about these lamb chops?"

"I don't want those."

"I made them for you."

"You didn't ask me."

"What am I supposed to do with them?"

"I don't care."

Her voice rose. "You don't *care*?"

"No."

"No?"

"I said no!"

"Neither do I!" she screamed and flung the frying pan

across the room. It clanged off the wall. We stood there staring in opposite directions, hearing only the sound of each other's angry breathing. We both knew we weren't talking about lamb chops.

"This is ridiculous," I finally mumbled.

"Maybe we should separate for a while," she said.

"Maybe we should," I said back.

NASSAU

LaPorta escorted Gianna Rule to a large hotel ballroom, the kind where convention groups hold their breakfasts. It was empty save for a few round tables, and the detective motioned his suspect to sit down. He went to close the door when he spotted Sampson running down the hallway, holding a large iPad.

"These just came through," he said, panting.

He handed the iPad to LaPorta, who grinned. Finally. The full security camera footage from Alfie's time at the roulette table.

"Let's see how she reacts to this," LaPorta said.

They approached the table where Gianna was busy texting on her phone and shaking her head. Why wasn't her assistant answering? She needed to tell the magazine folks she was delayed, although she didn't want to say why. She didn't *know* why.

"All right," LaPorta said, pulling out a chair. "Sorry to keep you waiting."

Gianna studied the man, who appeared to be in his early fifties. American. Mustached. A tad overweight. He wore a tan button-down shirt and a forest-green tie but had no badge or uniform, unlike the police officer standing behind him.

"My name is Detective LaPorta," he began.

"OK . . ." Gianna said slowly.

"I work for the casino."

"I've never been there."

"Do you want to tell me about the wire transfer?"

"What wire transfer?"

"The two million dollars."

Her eyes widened. "Two million dollars? I don't have two million dollars to send anyone!"

"It was sent to *you*."

"To me?" She laughed. "I don't think so."

"I do."

"When?"

"Yesterday."

She pushed back in her chair.

"Honestly, I don't know what you're talking about."

There it is, LaPorta thought. *Just like Alfie predicted.*

"The money was sent by someone you know."

"Who?"

"Why don't *you* tell *me*?"

"I don't have a clue, Officer."

"Detective. I'm a detective." He nodded toward Sampson. "He's an officer."

"Well, Detective—and Officer—I'm afraid you've made a mista—"

"The money came from Alfie Logan."

She froze for a moment. Then her head dropped, as if she were being pranked. She ran a hand through her hair, looked up, and smiled broadly.

"Now I *know* you've made a mistake."

"Why?"

"Alfie Logan doesn't have two million dollars. Or anything close."

"He won it."

Her eyes narrowed. "Where?"

"Here."

LaPorta froze an image on the iPad and handed it over. Gianna gazed at the photo of various people around a roulette table.

"Isn't that your ex-husband?"

Gianna frowned and exhaled.

"Oh, God, it is," she mumbled. "I heard he was in town."

LaPorta leaned forward.

"You want to tell us how he won the money?"

"Who?"

"Your ex."

"I thought you said Alfie won the money."

"Yeah. Alfie. Your ex."

"*Alfie?*" She laughed loudly. "Alfie and I were never married. God, no!"

She pointed to a man in the photo standing alongside the roulette wheel.

"Mike. That's my ex."

Six

THE COMPOSITION BOOK

Things my mother said she loved about me:

11.   "The way you pray."

I think a lot about heaven these days. The dying often do. I wonder, if there is such a place, will I be overcome with its magnificence as others are? Or am I destined to experience things differently? The allure of heaven is that it's a second chance, right? But I have had second chances all my life. They've only left me with a failure to appreciate.

When Gianna and I separated, I told her I would find a place to live nearby, but I knew I wasn't going to stay in New York. I took what money I had out of the bank and headed straight for the airport, where I began a long journey of risk-taking adventures, hoping to erase my wife's haunting looks of disappointment. This was when I still believed that a heart could be distracted from itself.

I flew to China and took a thirty-hour train ride through the Gobi Desert, following the Silk Road trade route. At one point in the mountains I disembarked and wandered off. I tried not to focus on Gianna, but I wasn't very successful. I kept wondering what she was doing without me. I turned when I heard a train approaching. Then, as if moving in a dream, I stepped onto the rails. I wasn't planning to kill myself. Just trying to empty my head.

I watched the train grow larger as it approached. I heard the horn, or alarm, or whatever they use, blasting at me. Only when I could make out a figure behind the front car glass did I holler *"Twice!"*—and was instantly back at the Xi'an railway station that morning, sitting on a blue plastic bench.

A minute later, I was thinking about Gianna again.

I repeated this failed daredevil bit in numerous spots around the world. I joined a mountain climbing group in the Pyrenees in Spain, and when we stopped to rest on a large crag, I quietly unhooked, turned from the others, and flung myself off the side. I remember how quickly their screams faded as I fell. I slammed my eyes shut while yelling *"Twice!,"* then opened them, safely back in my tent that morning.

There was a great white shark encounter in Australia that still kind of haunts me (they are terrifying creatures, even if you know you can escape them) and a foolhardy motorcycle jump in the Philippines. When tempting death failed to move me, I tried a monastery in Malaysia for three months, to see if doing nothing was the answer. A waste of time. I thought of Gianna through most of the meditations. And the food was lousy.

During this long, ruminating walkabout, I met many people. I made small talk, ate meals, even went to bars with a few of them. There were plenty of women to connect with—backpackers, local workers, vacationers, escapees from the rat race—but I stayed away from relationships. I didn't want to complicate matters with Gianna. I kept my wedding ring on my finger.

But I *was* lonely. Now and then, if I spotted a woman I found particularly alluring, I'd find myself thinking not about my wife, but about Nicolette Pink and that moment in the elevator, with her suggestive purring as she undid my belt. I visualized it more than I should have. I missed Gianna's tenderness. But I fantasized about Nicolette. A split had formed in my heart. And here is another Truth About True Love: only a whole heart can support it.

I finally decided to go back to Africa and see what had become of the village where my family once lived. It took me a while to find it, but once I got there, I was pleasantly surprised. It had grown some, and the plumbing in the buildings had improved. But the cinnamon dirt soccer field was still there, as was the small church, and overall it hadn't changed that much, given the thirty years that had passed. No one remembered me except the village pastor, who smiled when he first saw me and leaned backward, as if looking at a skyscraper.

"How tall you have become!" he said.

He was completely bald now, with a gray beard that reached his chest, but he still wore a tweed jacket over his clerical collar. And he still had a goat. A different goat.

"Your father?"

"He's good, yeah."

"And your church back home?"

"Yeah, also good, thanks." I was lying. I hadn't been there in decades.

"We were blessed to have your mother with us for the

time she was here, and we are still sorry she went to our Lord so soon."

"Yeah," I mumbled.

"Come and pray with me, Alfie," he said.

I followed him into the small church, and he knelt and recited his devotions in Swahili. He ended with the "Our Father," and nodded to me to join in English. I hadn't said it in years, but I still remembered every word. When we finished—"for thine is the kingdom and the power and the glory, forever and ever, amen"—the pastor looked over and whispered, "Well done, Alfie," and I choked up because my mother used to say the same thing. I thought about what she and my grandmother had both told me before they died: "I want, and you want, and God does what God wants."

Was this what God wanted? My meandering life?

*

Before I left, I asked the pastor if he still let the village kids ride an elephant on Saturdays. He grinned and said, "Oh, yes, Lallu still amuses them."

"Lallu is still around?"

"Of course. Elephants live a long time."

I wanted to see for myself, so I caught a jeep ride out to the farm. To my surprise, I still recognized the owner, who was standing on his porch, leaning on a long cane. When I said "Lallu," he pointed to his son, who was working on a nearby tractor engine. He looked to be about my age and was wearing a tight yellow soccer shirt and lime-green basketball shorts. When I introduced myself, he looked up, a toothpick in his mouth.

"American?"

"Yes. I lived here as a boy."

"Why?"

"Missionary work."

"You teach my people God?"

"My parents."

"You should teach them money. That what we need. Money now. God later."

"OK."

"You have money?"

"Not really, no."

A fly buzzed between us. He swatted it away.

"My name is Alfie."

"Juma."

I offered my hand, which he looked at, then shook weakly.

"You want elephant?"

"I'd like to see Lallu, yes. I used to play with her."

He rolled the toothpick in his teeth.

"You want to buy her?"

"Buy Lallu?"

"You have money?"

"I can't buy an elephant."

He made a snick sound with his mouth. "Elephant worth a lot."

"To who?"

He stared for a moment, then gave up on the conversation. He nodded to his left, and I followed him past a large shed and rows of cassava and mango trees. Surrounding them were makeshift wooden fences, and on every post was a yellow box full of bees, designed to keep elephants away.

Juma slapped his shoe in the dirt and kicked at some stones. We walked for a few more minutes until I heard the sound of snapping branches. And suddenly, there she was— Lallu, standing beside a large tamarind tree.

There are no words for when an elephant first comes into your view. Only that your eyes widen and your heartbeat accelerates. Lallu's ears were longer than I remembered, and her massive back more hollow. But it was her.

I instinctively froze in place. Elephants have an incredible sense of smell, so I knew she'd already picked up my scent. And I knew to let her react before I did. Her ears moved slightly. She took a few plodding steps forward.

Juma watched curiously. Soon, Lallu was just a few feet away. She lifted her trunk and uncurled it into my chest. It should have frightened me, but it didn't. Knowing I could time jump if things got dangerous helped. But honestly, it felt so *familiar*. Lallu ran her trunk along my head then behind my shoulders. She seemed to be nudging me toward her. I eased in and she made a soft noise. Juma laughed.

"She remember you, man."

"You think so?"

"Listen. She telling you."

I felt myself smiling broadly, flushed with a nostalgic joy that came rushing back like a kid running to greet a parent at the airport. I edged closer into Lallu's massive legs, and she wrapped her trunk under my arms.

And in that unexpected embrace, my soul seemed to melt and my need to wander melted, too. I took in the feel of her scaly skin, and the long blue African sky above us, and the sticky heat, and the smell of the dirt, and I flashed back on my many Saturdays here, and my mother, who had come to this place to do good, to be better, and a little girl named Princess who brought me red mabuyu sweets. I was suddenly overcome by a yearning, if not a grief, for my once-innocent childhood, before I had the power to undo the Lord's timelines. On a calendar, it was thirty years since my days here, but with all my jumps and life corrections, who knew how long it had really been? Or how old I actually was? Lallu and I shared a memory that almost no one else in the world could: the version of me before I became different.

Gianna shared it, too. I remembered as kids when she said we should move here and build a house by the sea. I realized how lucky I was to have her in my life. Of all the things that had happened to me twice, she was the best.

I blinked back tears. I looked up into Lallu's small, steady eyes, and understood another Truth About True Love: it makes you feel like you belong someplace.

"I need to go home now, Lallu," I whispered.

Juma spit out the toothpick.

"Why you talk to her, man?" he said. "She don't understand you."

But I think she did.

*

I was back in New York a week later. I could have called Gianna to say I wanted to see her, but it had been months, and I didn't want to start things back over the phone. I got a room at a hotel and took a long hot shower. Since all my clothes were filthy from my travels, I stopped at a department store and bought new underwear and socks and jeans and a decent shirt. Then I grabbed a cab to our apartment building, took the elevator up, and stood outside the door.

I sucked in a few breaths, excited to see her to the point of giddiness. I had an apology practiced. And a new sense of patience. Mostly, I just planned to tell her how much I loved her, and promise to show her, to do better, to be better. I gripped an envelope with some photos of Lallu that Juma had taken, and I knocked.

No answer.

For a fleeting moment, I wondered if she'd moved. I knocked again, loudly. Nothing. I still had my key. I fished it from my wallet and tried the lock. It worked. I let myself in.

The place was the same, but I could feel my absence everywhere. All the possessions were Gianna's. Her sweater on the couch. Her sunglasses on the counter. Her purse. Her magazines. None of my coffee cups in the sink, or jackets on the back of a chair.

I waited a few minutes, then started to feel like I was trespassing. I removed a single photo from the envelope, Lallu and me, with her trunk pushing my hat over my eyes. I placed it on the coffee table, imagining it a small surprise for Gianna. I had my hand on the door, about to leave, when I heard the sound of the elevator opening down the hallway, and then her voice, animated, saying "I couldn't believe it, you know?" I heard a response from another voice, a man's voice, and I retreated, suddenly trapped, and before I could do anything the door was swinging open and I was looking straight across at a stunned Gianna, wearing a lavender turtleneck and a leather coat and standing in front of a guy whose face was instantly familiar from my freshman year at college.

Mike.

The soccer star. The guitar player. The guy who'd broken her heart.

"Alfie!" she screamed. "Oh my God! What are you doing here?"

"*Twice*," I whispered.

*

Now, Boss, if you're hoping for an explanation of what Gianna was doing with her old boyfriend, I don't have one. You'd have to ask her. I time jumped back to, of all places, the department store fitting room, where I was breathing hard and cursing until a salesman on the other side of the curtain said, "Sir, are you all right in there?"

I spent the next hour weighing whether I should return to the scene and confront Gianna. She was still my wife, after all. I thought of every possible reason why she could be coming to our apartment with her old college beau, but my mind kept returning to the worst one, that she was seeing him again, that she was sleeping with him.

That I had been replaced.

I knew if I revisited the moment, I could not undo it. I'd be stuck inside the apartment, staring at Mike and his perfect teeth and two-day stubble, and forced to have my confrontation with Gianna in front of him. I didn't want that. But I couldn't just leave things. I needed to know more. So I took a cab back to our apartment building and found a spot across the street, in a Korean grocery store. I positioned myself by the window. And I waited.

I must have looked at my watch a thousand times. I scanned the faces of everyone who came down the block. New York City is an endless cast of characters, pouring out of taxis, pushing through doorframes, turning around the corners. I wasn't sure if I'd missed Gianna by looking the wrong way at the wrong moment.

But then a bus stopped at a nearby intersection, and I caught sight of her stepping off. There was Mike right behind her. They walked together, heads nodding in intermittent conversation. They stopped momentarily by a vendor selling mixed nuts, but Gianna shook her head, and they continued on. I kept waiting for her to look my way. What was I hoping? That she'd break into tears? Push Mike away and come running with her arms out, screaming, "Alfie! You're back!"

They approached our building, and from behind, I saw Gianna reach into her handbag, maybe looking for her key. Mike turned his head. Then he made a small gesture that is forever seared in my memory.

He put his arm around Gianna's shoulder, and when he did, Gianna patted her free hand on his. If a single human act could morph into an arrow, that one would have shot directly across the street, shattered the glass of the grocery window, and pierced my heart.

My throat constricted. I started to sweat. When you experience an emotion you've never felt before, your body is confused. And in my mind I had just, for the first time in my life, lost someone I truly loved—not to the angel of death, but to another person's affection. Where do I go? What do I do? Beneath my suddenly uncomfortable skin, my soul felt gutted, angry, pathetic, victimized.

And at fault.

"Ey! Mister! *Mister!*"

I turned. The Korean owner was scowling from behind the cash register.

"You buy or leave! No stand there. Buy or leave!"

Buy or leave. That's what it felt like. Invest in whatever

it would take to get Gianna back—long talks, long apologies, new promises, new behavior—or walk away, licking my wounds.

I walked away.

*

What happened next, Boss, I am not proud of. I went to a liquor store, bought four bottles of whiskey, and marched back to the hotel. I stayed there for two nights, ripping up photos of Lallu and drinking myself into a stupor. I didn't eat. I barely slept. Late on the second night, half out of my head, I called Gianna's number from the room phone.

It was well past midnight. The answering machine picked up. We used to have a dumb message, the two of us trading lines, then finishing by screaming "Beeeeep!" But now I heard her recorded voice, solo, calm, saying *"Hi, it's Gianna, sorry I missed you, leave a message."*

The words played tricks in my head. *Sorry. I missed you.* I pressed the receiver to my ear, breathing hard, maybe even crying. *Sorry. I missed you.* And then I heard a sudden fumbling noise, as if she knocked the phone over trying to answer it.

I panicked and hung up.

In that moment, my worst imagination took over. I pictured Gianna and Mike in bed, making love, ignoring the ringing (*Should you get that?* Mike whispers, *No, nooo*, Gianna moans) until my whimpering could no longer be ignored and Gianna, naked, stretched for the phone and knocked it over. And, as I pathetically hung up, the two of them burst into laughter, then flung themselves back atop one another.

It was a stupid, agonizing thought at a stupid, agonizing moment. But I have already made my case about moments: how you forget so many over a lifetime, yet a lifetime can turn on a single one.

At that low moment, fueled with alcohol, jealousy, and the relentless ache of being no longer wanted, I thought back to a time when the tables were turned, when I was the desired one. I thought back to Nicolette, beautiful, sexy Nicolette, and the night I left her in that elevator in L.A. The memory glowed in my mind like a lighthouse tugging me from the fog.

With my eyes squeezed closed, wanting only relief from the hurt, I inhaled the deepest breath I'd ever taken on this earth, and screamed out *"Twice!"*

Instantly, I was back in that elevator, with Nicolette's hands on my belt, undoing it slowly while she purred, "Lemme see. Lemme see . . ."

This time, I let her see. I let her do everything she wanted. In that elevator. In her luxurious hotel suite. Across her king-size mattress. Against the bedroom wall. I summoned every ounce of my virility that night and lost myself inside her supple body, because losing myself was what I wanted to do.

Sadly, when you lose yourself, you don't realize who else you're losing, too.

NASSAU

LaPorta tapped his finger on the iPad photo.

"*That's* your ex-husband?" he said, pointing to a man standing by the roulette wheel.

"Yes," Gianna said.

"And this guy is not?"

"That's Alfie."

"Who has never been married to you?"

"No!"

"He never met you in Africa?"

"He did. When we were kids."

"He didn't go to college with you?"

"Yes. Well. Not *with* me. We were at the same school."

"He never told you he loved you? Made a big deal about it during a rainstorm in Philadelphia?"

"Look, Detective, I don't know what you're—"

"Never married you in some little town? Never fought with you over having a baby?"

Gianna straightened her back. She looked upset.

"I don't want to talk to you anymore. Not until I have a lawyer."

"Look, lady, I'm not trying—"

"My name is Gianna Rule. Not 'lady.' And I don't know what you have against Alfie, or why you would make all this up, but it's not fair to him, and I'm not putting up w—"

"He ripped off a casino."

"He doesn't gamble! That's not Alfie! He's a good man. He doesn't take stupid chances."

LaPorta leaned back. "You'd be surprised."

Gianna shook her head.

"I'm not saying anything more. Not until I have representation. I'm an American citizen. I have the right to—"

"I know all about your rights," LaPorta interrupted. "I also know there's two million dollars in a bank account that bears your name. And it came from this guy in the photo, after an impossible three straight ups at a roulette table, which can only be done by cheating, which is illegal. So, you might not want to talk to me . . ."

He leaned over and opened his bag. He pulled out a notebook.

"But you're gonna want to read this."

THE COMPOSITION BOOK

I stayed in Mexico with Nicolette for the remaining two months of the movie shoot. We were discreet around the set, never more than sitting together behind a camera. But at night, it was a different story. I would knock on her hotel room door, and she'd swing it open, wearing a robe, look both ways down the hall, then pull me in and push me toward her huge bed, undressing me as she kissed my face and dropped the robe to reveal nothing underneath. Our lovemaking was intense and noisy, rooted in pleasure and sensation. At times, it seemed that Nicolette was enjoying how good she was at it, even as she was enjoying me.

I didn't care. Yes, it was different from when Gianna and I were together, which was more about emotion and eye contact and holding each other afterward, tender and content. But anytime I thought of that, I pictured her with Mike, and my body tightened like a sprinter in the final strides of a race. I threw myself into satisfying this seductive woman who was coiled around me, and I didn't think about anything else.

I would never spend the night in Nicolette's bed, because the production assistants came by early in the morning, and she didn't want to risk us getting caught. But we did talk a good deal, often over late-night room service. We traded stories about our childhoods, our careers, our parents. Nicolette's father had been abusive, and she ran away from home when she was fifteen. Her mother, she said, stopped taking her calls for years—until she appeared in her first movie.

"Then, suddenly, she was telling the neighbors about me," Nicolette said.

"That's awful."

"What about your mother? How'd she treat you?"

"She was great. I loved every minute I had with her."

"She died when you were young, right?"

"Eight."

"That's so sad. I'm sorry, Alfie."

I looked in her eyes. She seemed genuinely empathetic.

"She gave me something before she died."

"What was it?"

"A gift. A magical talent."

She made a sly smile, then lifted her leg and rubbed her foot around my thigh.

"What kind of talent?" she cooed.

She leaned over and began kissing my neck. That was as close as I came to telling her the truth. We spent one weekend at a resort along the coast, and another weekend in Cancún. During those escapes, she was less guarded, and we sometimes walked hand in hand along a beach, or swam together in a pool. She never really asked about Gianna, but I volunteered that things were not good between us and that we had separated. I was mixing years, of course. During that time, Gianna was actually still in New York, in our apartment, and we hadn't yet tried having a baby, hadn't yet fought over that failure, hadn't yet taken a "break," or had a surprise confrontation with her old boyfriend standing behind her.

Didn't matter. I knew it would happen. And I was living the way I had always lived, with many lifetimes snaggled around each other. The truth is, I told myself where Gianna was going, so I could excuse where I was.

*

At the beginning, I had called Gianna every night from Mexico, telling her about the daily movie activity and lying about why they needed me there. By the end of the shoot, we only spoke every couple of days.

One night, after some particularly wild lovemaking with Nicolette, followed by grilled cheese sandwiches and a bottle of wine, I was leaving her room when, wearing just a cropped T-shirt and panties, she grabbed me close, tipsy, and nuzzled her cheek against mine. "Sing me something," she said. So I softly sang another verse from "Make Someone Happy," the song I knew she liked:

> *"One smile that cheers you*
> *One face that lights when it nears you*
> *One girl you're everything to."*

She made a satisfied groan when I finished, and as I opened the door to leave she kissed me gently on the lips and said, "Mmm, love you," and I instinctively replied, "I love you, too."

*

Now, Boss, comes the tragic part. It will make sense once you read it, and maybe then you will grant my last request regarding Gianna. I hope so. It's all I have left.

I returned to New York once the movie finished shooting. Gianna left a message saying she was stuck at work and couldn't make it to the airport, could I get a cab into the city? That was different. Usually, if I went away, even for a few days, Gianna would be waiting at the gate, holding snacks in case I was hungry and jumping up and down as if she hadn't seen me in a year.

I used the cab ride to set my composure. How was I going to handle our reunion? I'd time jumped back nearly three years to Mexico because I'd been angry at Gianna, and Mike, and that whole confrontation. And once in the past, I'd been narrow-minded in my emotions. Nicolette and I were making a film during the day and making love at night. I selfishly made no room for outside thoughts about my wife or our future. Maybe because I knew, deep down, I'd acted rashly. I didn't want to face that.

But back in New York, everything felt different, as if a summer had ended and I'd returned to a sterile classroom. Nicolette was off to make a film in Canada, so there was no seeing her for a while. We hadn't formalized anything, other than to say we would miss one another and I would try to fly out to see her during her shoot.

As I waited for Gianna to return, I wandered around the

apartment, remembering my last time here, three years in the future, when we'd already separated and my presence had been erased.

But now my coffee mugs were on the kitchen counter and my shoes were in the closet and it hit me that I was about to relive not days or months, but the longest stretch I had ever repeated in my life. While I'd known this intellectually, I don't think I absorbed it emotionally until that moment, staring at my old sneakers.

"Hey, hi," Gianna said, pushing through the door. "You're home. How was it?"

The first thing I noticed was her tone, which was different. Flatter. Her hair was cut short, the way she'd worn it back then. But her usual smile was missing.

"It was good. Good. Tiring." I injected more enthusiasm into my voice. "How are *you* doing?"

I stepped forward and initiated a kiss, which she returned. I can't say if it was my lips or hers, but something had changed.

"I'm fine," she said.

"What's been going on?"

"You know. Same stuff."

"Yeah."

There was a pause that lasted a couple seconds. It felt like a decade.

"You hungry?" she said.

"Um . . . yeah. Yeah. Let's go out."

"I have some food here."

"All right. We can eat here."

"OK."

"OK."

"Give me a second to get cleaned up."

"Yeah."

She hung up her coat and headed to the bathroom.

"Gianna?"

She turned her head.

"It's nice to be home."

She nodded. "That's good," she said.

It was anything but.

*

Love is different, my grandmother had warned. *It's the only thing you can't do twice.*

I did remember that conversation, Boss. But time had worn down its urgency. Maybe I thought it didn't apply to me. Maybe I just wanted to think that.

At first, with Gianna, I blamed our new dynamic on the length of my absence. When you're gone a long time, it takes a while to readjust. We didn't make love my first night back, citing exhaustion, nor did we the next two nights, going to bed at different times. When we finally did, that weekend, it felt familiar, but almost obligatory. I admit, comparing it to the passion of Nicolette in a Mexican hotel room wasn't fair to my wife. But then, none of this was.

I thought back to that visit with my grandmother, when she held her photo album and teared up at the image of an old flame.

This woman. Gianna. Is it true love?

I think it is.

Then I'm worried, Alfie.

About what?

That you'll do something stupid.

Had I done that? Had I angered the force that granted me this power? Even writing that makes me sound like I was a victim, when the truth was, whatever I had done, I had done to myself. But my habit of fixing things had made me think I could fix this, too. I didn't realize how wrong I was until a month after I'd been home, when the consequence of my wandering heart became clear.

Gianna and I had re-immersed ourselves in old routines, seeing friends, going to movies. We were cordial enough. When I asked her "Is everything all right?" her answer was always "Fine."

Then, on a Monday night, we were sitting on the couch, when a commercial came on the TV for a household cleaner. It showed babies making a big mess of things, paint on their faces, soup in their laps, a litter box they'd overturned.

"Cute kids," I said.

Gianna nodded silently.

"What are you thinking?" I asked.

"Nothing."

"About children?"

She shrugged.

I knew from experience she was yearning for a family. I also knew it was dangerous to bring this up, because it had led to all the things that had unraveled us the first time. But trying to find my way through the smoke, I stepped into the fire.

"Do you want us to try for a baby?" I asked.

I saw her wince. Just slightly. But I saw it. A resistance? A repulsion? I had never seen that look before. My insides collapsed.

She hooked her hands together and dropped them in her lap.

"Alfie," she said, "we need to talk..."

But we didn't need to. I already knew. Yaya had been right. *If you change your mind, your first love will never love you again.*

Gianna was gone.

NASSAU

LaPorta hurried past the shooting fountains and into the casino, moving briskly past the blackjack tables and the clanging slot machines. He'd hated enduring the Nassau traffic again, but he needed to run the footage past Toussaint, the dealer who was first approached about the roulette scheme.

He unlocked the security office and saw two officers leaning against the wall, while Toussaint sat in a folding chair, chomping nervously on a piece of gum.

"Look at this," LaPorta said, pushing the iPad under his gaze. "Which one of these is the guy who approached you?"

Toussaint didn't hesitate.

"This man here."

LaPorta threw his head back in frustration. The ex-husband. Mike.

"*That's* the guy with the earring you were talking about?"

"Yes."

"Not this guy?"

He pointed to Alfie, sitting at the table. Toussaint squinted.

"I don't know this man."

"Ahhh, damn it!"

LaPorta banged his fist so hard on the table, Toussaint bounced in his seat.

"I want this footage circulated to every security person

here!" LaPorta yelled at the guards. "We need to find this guy fast. His name is Mike Kurtz. American. Move!"

The two guards rose quickly and LaPorta followed them out. Five minutes later, he was back in the squad car, returning to Gianna Rule, who at that very moment was hunched over a ballroom table, reading a notebook, with a hand on her mouth and tears coming down her face.

*

Alfie, now in handcuffs, was led down a corridor inside Fox Hill Prison. The walls were painted beige on top and dark green on the bottom, and oversized fans blew from the ceiling, creating a constant rumble. As the island's only correctional facility, the place was divided into maximum, medium, and minimum-security sections.

A guard directed him to the receiving desk, where Alfie stood as his papers were processed. He eyed a nearby emergency exit and took note of the security cameras' placements. The officer behind the desk wore a sand-colored uniform. He made a copy of Alfie's passport, then pointed to where the guard was to take him next.

"Excuse me," Alfie said. "But I am allowed a phone call under Bahamian law, right?"

The officer sighed.

"Yes, that is correct."

"I'd like to make it now, please."

"To family only, or your embassy."

"Understood."

Alfie was led to a counter with a telephone. The guard removed his handcuffs, then stood nearby.

"Could I have some privacy?" Alfie said.

The guard looked to the officer, who shrugged.

"He's minimum security. It doesn't matter."

The guard stepped away. Alfie dialed a number. It wasn't family. And it wasn't the embassy.

"Hello?"

"Have you found Gianna yet, Detective?"

"Alfie?" LaPorta's voice said, angrily. "How are you calling me? Where's your guard?"

"Relax. I'm at the jail. I'm doing what you want. Did you find Gianna?"

"You better put that guard on right now or I swear I'll have the police hunting you down—"

"Just tell me, and I'll put him on."

"Alfie, damn it—"

"Tell me, Vincent."

"Yes, she's reading your damn notebook right now! Put the guard on or so help me—"

"*Twice.*"

Alfie was suddenly back handcuffed again, as the man behind the desk made a copy of his passport.

"Excuse me. But I am allowed a phone call under Bahamian law, right?"

The officer sighed.

"Yes, that is correct."

Alfie nodded.

"Do you want to make it now?"

"Maybe later," Alfie said, smiling.

*

By the time LaPorta got back to the resort, he had a mountain of questions for Gianna Rule. What was the connection between Alfie and her ex-husband? If this guy Mike was behind the scam, why was Alfie playing the numbers? And why would Alfie call her his wife if they'd never been married?

Actually, that was just the start of LaPorta's questions. This case was like a maze, where you can walk for hours and never know if you're advancing or retreating. He rushed past the check-in desk and the gold elevators. He jogged down the corridor to the ballroom and pushed through the doors with a loud noise.

The security guard nodded at him, but Gianna Rule never looked up from the table. LaPorta noticed that the notebook was closed. And that she was crying.

"You finished it?" LaPorta said.

Gianna shook her head no.

"How much did you read?"

"Enough," she rasped.

"Why are you so upset?"

She squeezed her lips in silence.

"Look, Ms. Rule," LaPorta said, trying to sound empathetic, "you've got to answer my questions if you want me to help. I need to know Alfie's connection to your ex. And why he's making all this stuff up about the two of you being married.

"And while I'm at it . . . Who the hell is this boss that he's writing this notebook to?"

Gianna sniffed in deeply.

"Don't you understand?" she whispered. "*I'm* his boss."

Seven

THE COMPOSITION BOOK

What is it about love that makes us think we can tame it, when all the while it is taming us?

Gianna went to stay with friends while I moved out of our apartment, saying it was better "if we didn't watch each other untangle." We'd had a few difficult heart-to-hearts, and the performance review that couples give each other before they split. We came to the usual conclusions, that we'd "grown apart" and there was no point blaming each other. She was less emotional about it than I had imagined, which gave me pause, since being unemotional was never Gianna's thing.

Still, at the time, I stubbornly refused to believe my magic was solely at fault, that my time jump back to Nicolette's arms had done this, that my grandmother's warning about lovers not being able to love you twice had woven its evil spell. Perhaps this was coming anyhow, I reasoned. People change.

As I loaded boxes into a small U-Haul I had rented, I let thoughts of returning to Nicolette become my salve, a numbing agent to the pain of leaving Gianna, the woman who, in a whimsical ceremony in a Pennsylvania forest, I had promised I would always love, and who'd promised me she would do the same.

I called Nicolette from a pay phone in Manhattan. She was in Canada, about to leave for the day's shooting. I mentioned that Gianna and I had finally split up.

"Oh, I'm sorry, Alfie."

"It was coming for a while."

"That's the worst."

"I'm glad I have you to talk to."

"Of course."

"You know, I've been thinking. I'm pretty tired of New York and the cold. I can write from anywhere. I might move out to L.A. now."

"Really?"

"Yeah. Would you like that?"

I regretted asking the moment I did.

"Sure," she said. "I mean, that would be great. I'm not there a lot, you know. With shoots and everything. But—"

"Right, right. I wouldn't be coming for you. I mean, of course, I want to be with you. That would be the cool part. But I'm not, you know . . . I'm not saying . . ."

I waited for her to add something. She didn't.

"*Twice,*" I mumbled.

The second time around, I never made the call. I told myself I would see her at the premiere, five months away. Better to talk in person.

*

During this time, I got myself in better shape. I watched what I ate, lost some weight, and went to a gym five mornings a week to do weight work. I know it's a cliché, Boss, that people take better care of themselves *after* a relationship ends. And it is strange that you'd rather make yourself attractive for the possibility of a love, than for one you already have. I suppose all of it goes back to the grass is always greener. I looked up that phrase once. Did you know it dates to a Greek poet in the first century BC? That's how long we've been making fools of ourselves.

As the premiere approached, I flew out to Los Angeles but this time with no return ticket. That night at the hotel, sitting on the bed, I realized the last time I had lived through this day, Gianna had told me she was pregnant. I'd gone to sleep thinking I was going to be a father and wore that idea through the next day's festivities like a heavy gauze covering my eyes.

This time felt different. But not better. To be honest, I felt kind of empty. As I rode in the car that the studio had provided, I tried to convince myself that meeting up with Nicolette after the film was over—as I'd promised last time but never done—would ease the sting of my collapse with Gianna. I rubbed my arms through my sports coat, feeling my newly tightened muscles.

The crowd was the same as last time, as was Nicolette's arrival in that silver lamé dress, parting the attendees like a speedboat through a lake. The cameras flashed incessantly. When we saw each other, we repeated what happened in the previous encounter.

She took my hand and gently rubbed her thumb across my palm.

"Hi," she said.

"Hi, Nicolette."

"I've missed you. Are you good?"

"Yeah. And you?"

"Everything's great."

This time, I preempted her leaning in and did it first, offering her previous words back to her.

"Let's go make someone happy," I whispered.

She blinked, as if confused, then pushed up a smile.

"I'll see you after?" she said.

I saw her after. But not the way I'd hoped.

*

The movie finished, there was wild applause, and Nicolette and a couple of the other actors went to the front of the theater and spoke a few words to the audience. Then they thanked Jaimie and Marisol, who sat up front and got a huge ovation, and "the real writer, Alfie Logan, who is also here." I waved.

Afterward, there was the usual pandemonium of people pushing and cutting and greeting one another. I tried to see where Nicolette was going. I'd kind of hoped she'd find me, but with so much attention on her, I guess it was difficult. I wiggled through the crowd to the front of the theater, where they'd told me I'd have a car waiting to go to an after-party. But there were about fifty cars waiting. Valet parkers were racing back and forth with keys. I shuffled impatiently, reading the placards in the windshields, hoping to see my name.

Suddenly, I heard a small roar and saw more cameras flashing. I spotted Nicolette being ushered to her limo. She was waving with one arm, but the other was draped around the waist of a tall, bearded man whom I recognized as an actor, an action hero type, although I couldn't remember his name. When they reached the curb, there was sudden yelling from photographers, and Nicolette turned, still arm in arm with her man, and they smiled and posed until someone yelled "A kiss! A kiss!" and Nicolette reached her hand across his cheek and planted a long, wet smooch on his lips while flashes illuminated their perfect coupling, as if their love created daylight.

I'll spare you the embarrassing details of my being discarded, Boss—the canceled dinners, the unanswered phone calls, the personal assistant who eventually emailed me letting me know that Nicolette was "heavily involved in a new project but appreciated the invitation to get together and wishes you well."

Eight months later, I read she was engaged to the action hero. They were making a big-budget "futuristic fantasy" film together. I laughed at the word *futuristic* because I had so badly estimated my future with her. Then again, I had only really turned to Nicolette after messing things up with Gianna. Maybe she never actually cared about me. Maybe I just misread everything.

Who knows? We invent all kinds of theories about how our hearts get broken, when we're the ones who drop them on the floor.

*

Now, if you're wondering if I ever contacted Gianna again, Boss, I did. A few times. I called her on the phone. I showed up at the camera store where she worked. She was never mean. But the spark was gone. Just like Yaya had experienced with George. I could see it in Gianna's forced smile. Her glances out the window. Her sentences like "I know things will get better for you, Alfie." Always "you." Never "us."

In time, I gave up. I moved down to Australia, which felt as far away as I could get, and I stayed there for many years. I took on physical jobs. I lived near a beach. I never married again.

Looking back, the story is pretty simple. I ignored my mother's warnings that the second time won't always be better, and I did the "something stupid" my Yaya had worried about. Somewhere in heaven, I broke both their hearts.

I walked away from my one true love, Boss. And the lone caveat of my unique gift—*You cannot get someone to love you twice*—meant I could never undo the biggest mistake of my life.

I have cursed this power ever since.

NASSAU

"What do you mean, *you're* his boss?"

LaPorta was shaking his head in confusion, like a man whose key no longer opens his front door.

"Alfie's been working with me for years," Gianna said. "He's my assistant. My right-hand person. He takes care of everything." Her voice softened. "He's kind of my best friend."

"Since when?"

"Since we got out of college."

"Wait. So you were in school together? That part's true?"

"Yes."

"What else?"

"We met in Africa as kids. We saw each other again in Miami. I did meet his grandmother once. Not the way he described. But the rest of it . . ."

She choked up. "Poor Alfie."

"Why 'poor Alfie'?"

"He's obviously not well. I knew there was something wrong with his health. He's been falling a lot. He's always tired. But I didn't know that his mind . . . I mean, his brain must be affected."

She lifted the notebook. "Why else would he write all this?"

LaPorta squeezed his fists. *No sympathy. Stay on the case. The two million bucks.*

"Was he in debt? Did he owe people?"

"Alfie?" Gianna almost laughed. "Not a chance. He stays in my guest house. He drives my old car. I've tried to increase his salary a hundred times. He always says he has everything he needs."

"What about your husband?"

"My ex-husband?"

"Yeah. Could they have cooked this up together?"

"No. No way." Gianna shook her head. "Alfie never liked Mike. Never trusted him. He tried to warn me about him." She paused. "I should've listened."

"Why?"

"Why do you think? Lies. Other women. Spending my money. Take your pick."

She flashed her eyes at LaPorta with a look that he recognized as weary heartbreak.

"When did you two divorce?"

"Ten years ago."

"Was it bad?"

"Awful. Mike fought me over everything. He even stalked me for a while. I had to take out a restraining order."

"You never married again?"

"God, no. Mike ruined that whole idea. Sadly, thanks to an idiot judge, he still has a piece of my business."

"What business?"

"Photography."

"That's a business?"

"I take pictures all over the world, Detective. I've published nine books. Done countless exhibits. I have two galleries, in New York and San Francisco. So yeah." She sighed. "It's a business."

"Sorry—"

"Doesn't matter."

"And your ex—"

"I made him a partner when we got married. Another mistake—on top of marrying him in the first place."

LaPorta reached in his pants pocket but realized he'd left his Life Savers behind. He desperately wanted a cigarette. Coffee. A drink. Anything. He dropped into a chair and tried to sum up the facts.

"So you have a lousy ex, who blows money. You have an employee who has crazy fantasies about you. These two guys don't like each other, but they're at a roulette table together the other night. Alfie wins the money, even though he doesn't need it, while your ex walks away with nothing. Then Alfie wires the money to you, and someplace in Africa. And when we arrest him, he says everything is explained in a notebook. How the hell does that make sense?"

"Africa?" Gianna said, leaning in. "Where in Africa?"

"Zimbabwe. Does that mean something to you?"

"No. I've never been there."

She leaned back. "Look, Detective. Alfie needs our help."

"Maybe. But first he's gonna confess what he did, return that money, and face the charges."

"He's innocent," Gianna said, staring at the notebook. "I know he is."

She thumbed the pages, then slowly let them fall. LaPorta

watched, trying to picture these two as soulmates, a happy couple, the way Alfie had described them.

"Can I ask you something?" LaPorta said.

"All right."

"Did you ever love him?"

Gianna's gaze drifted. "Not like that."

"Well. He obviously loved you. Or still does."

LaPorta rose.

"Where are you going?" Gianna asked.

"To find your ex. And everyone else around that roulette table."

"Wait." She put her hand on the notebook cover. "Don't you think we should finish this?"

LaPorta couldn't fathom the idea of reading any more fantasy.

"Knock yourself out," he said. "But you're still a suspect, Ms. Rule." He nodded to the guard. "She doesn't leave this room. Got it?"

THE COMPOSITION BOOK

I'd never seen the movie *Alfie*, Boss. Not until recently. I guess I was so tired of people singing that song to me—*What's it all about, Alfie?*—I never wanted to bother.

I had been living Down Under for decades. I'd developed into a pretty good carpenter, plumber, electrician, what the Aussies call "a ripper." I made enough money to cover my needs and lived a fairly healthful life, lots of walks and fruit drinks and swimming in the ocean. I rented a flat near the beach. Two bedrooms. A decent kitchen with a dishwasher. And plenty of private storage in the basement, which I used for my massive collection of notebooks—although I wasn't as meticulous in my record-keeping anymore. There wasn't much I wanted to repeat.

I won't bore you with the details of those many years, Boss. I lived. I worked. I slept. I drank with the locals. I played piano on Sundays in a nearby church, which would have made my mother happy. I had a couple of health blips. Nothing too serious.

As far as romantic relationships, well, they started and they ended. I never misled anyone, always saying I wasn't a forever type. The truth was, after Gianna, I shut down my heart. Women picked up on this quickly. Those who did bother to share their beds with me had their own built-in departure clocks. I was left more often than I did the leaving. Didn't matter. After all that had transpired, none of it really hurt me.

I got diagnosed with my disease late last year. Then, earlier this month, I had a stroke. It's hard to describe that, Boss. I was painting a client's patio and had just stepped off a ladder when I got dizzy. My head began buzzing. I had been holding a paint can with my left hand and I don't remember dropping it, but when I glanced down the can was rolling away and my foot was covered in buttercup yellow. I fell in the driveway. My face hit the concrete. My arm went numb. I heard people yelling, but it sounded like they were underwater.

I woke up in the hospital.

My left side was unresponsive. I had bruises on my face and elbow. Worst of all, I couldn't speak. I had to listen helplessly as nurses and doctors asked me to blink if I understood what they were saying. They read the records of my diagnosis, and the chief doctor said, "That likely increased your chances of an incident." Yeah. No kidding.

Anyhow, I was there for a week or so when an older nurse, who noticed no one was coming to visit, entered my room and said she had something for me. She held up a DVD.

"It's called *Alfie*," she said. "Have you seen it?"

I shook my head slightly, which was all I could do.

"I noticed it on the shelf of discs we keep for patients. I thought, with your name, maybe you'd want to watch it."

I blinked OK. What else was I doing?

She put it in the player. It came up on the TV screen. She touched my arm, smiled, and left. And finally, after all those years, I watched the film about the person whose name I shared.

It was horrible.

The story was cruel. The main character was despicable. For some reason, I thought Alfie would be a lovable playboy who you rooted for through his romances. No. He was a cad. A louse. Insensitive. Mean. Referring to women as "birds." Leaving them as soon as they developed feelings for him. He said his understanding of females only extended to their pleasure. When it came to their pain, he didn't want to know.

I realize it's just a movie, Boss, but as it went along, I felt worse and worse about myself. Maybe because I kept hearing female characters call the name "Alfie!" in frustration. Lying there, motionless, I thought about the various deceptions I had used with the opposite sex, from young Adrian and our kiss in the closet, to high schoolers like Natalie and Jo Ann Donnigan and Lizzie, to college women like Maisie and Danielle, to Nicolette Pink, and, of course, mostly, to Gianna. The woman who told me "destiny is patient."

I had tried, over the years, to put our relationship in a box and hide that box somewhere far from my heart. But in that hospital bed, with Alfie cavorting on the screen, the memories of what I'd had and what I'd lost came back with a fury. I wanted the film to stop, but I couldn't reach the remote. I couldn't call out.

So it kept playing until the final scene, when Alfie turns to the audience and delivers the summary of his existence. He says when he looked back on how he'd behaved, especially with women, you'd think he'd gotten the best of it.

But what did he really gain? He kept his freedom. But he had no peace of mind. And without that, he had nothing.

"So, what's the answer?" he wonders in the final lines. "That's what I keep asking myself—what's it all about?"

Then that familiar song starts playing. By the time it did, tears were streaming down my face. I tried lamely to swat them away with my one good hand. And I wondered if this was how I would spend my final moments on earth, alone, with no one who cared about me, in a sterile hospital room, the only sounds being the muted conversations of strangers in a hallway.

What's it all about, Alfie? After all these years, it turns out that lyric was referring to a sad, lonely, pathetic man. A man without love. I wept in that hospital bed, because I had become my namesake.

*

Now I will add these final paragraphs.

I have been writing this notebook story for a long time, Boss. To confess. To explain. But mostly to say I am sorry, beyond sorry, for the foolish things I did to you. To us. To our love. I beg your forgiveness.

I have said my stroke happened this month. And it did. This month—in another lifetime. I went back and repeated many decades. But they have passed now, and that stroke is looming again. It will hit me very soon, and my voice will be gone. I had planned for you to read these pages after I died. But things have changed, and there is still much to tell you.

I have lived today more than once. The Bahamas. The casino. Being arrested. Detective LaPorta, who, despite his bluster, I sort of like. All of it, up to the moment that this notebook is about to be taken from me and, I can only pray, winds up in your hands.

If it has, if you have read this far, then this is my final request: let me finish this story in front of you. There is a landmark here on the island called the Queen's Staircase. I will be there tonight, at 11:30. Don't worry about how I escape custody; you can do a lot when you know what's going to happen.

The Queen's Staircase.

Please come, Gianna.

I can explain everything if you do.

If you choose not to, if this is all too much, I understand. I have lived a lifetime with you just out of reach. I can die that way as well.

NASSAU

Mike Kurtz had been sitting at Gate 9 of the Lynden Pindling International Airport, awaiting a flight to Miami, when security identified him. He was handcuffed and driven to a police station in downtown Nassau.

Around the same time, the roulette croupier, whose name was Solomon Augustin, was arrested returning to his apartment two blocks off Bay Street.

Both men, and Toussaint, the Haitian casino dealer, were questioned in separate rooms by Vince LaPorta.

The croupier again denied knowing Alfie. But he reacted differently when asked about Mike Kurtz. With a prior misdemeanor on his record, he was worried about a second offense. He agreed to confess in exchange for leniency.

"Talk," LaPorta said.

The croupier said that Kurtz and two cohorts had approached him with a proposition. They'd managed to get a magnet under a roulette wheel in the casino and wanted him to slip a special ball in it during a moment when the security cameras were blocked. In exchange, they offered the croupier a large cut of their winnings.

"How did this ball work?" LaPorta asked.

"A computer chip inside. And magnets, one in the ball, one outside."

"Where was the outside magnet?"

"Mike wore it."

"Where?"

The croupier tapped his hip. "Under his pants. If he stands close enough, and the man with the computer programs it right, the magnet pulls the ball to the number they bet."

LaPorta rubbed his forehead. He had heard of magnet use, but computer chips were a new frontier. This was high-level cheating. He wondered how he was going to stay ahead of it.

"So where does Alfie Logan fit in this?"

"Who?"

LaPorta banged his finger on the iPad photo.

"The guy who placed the bets! The guy who won the money! Him!"

"I told you, I don't know that man! He comes from nowhere, sits down, and plays the numbers that this Mike guy programmed."

"But the footage never shows Mike Kurtz betting."

"He wasn't supposed to. His partner was. But when this man—what's his name?"

"Alfie—"

"When this Alfie put so many chips on that number, Mike's man got scared. When he did it again, Mike got scared, too. He called it off. They left."

"That's it?"

"Yes. You see? Nothing happened. I am innocent."

"You put a loaded ball into a rigged roulette wheel. That's not innocent."

But LaPorta's mind wasn't on charging the croupier. He still had no answer for Alfie's actions.

"What about the third time? When Alfie won the two million?"

"I told you! I don't know nothing about this Alfie!"

LaPorta rose, yanked open the door, and marched down the hall. He pushed into another interrogation room, where Mike Kurtz was seated, rapping his knuckles on a table. He was tall, muscular, and unshaven, with dark, thinning hair and an earring. His shirt was one of those flower print things tourists buy in overpriced hotel shops.

"Alfie Logan!" LaPorta barked. "What's your connection with him?"

Kurtz scowled. "Don't ask me about that prick."

"Why not? He won the money you were supposed to win. With your magnetized ball."

Kurtz sneered. "I don't know what you're talking about."

"We know what you did, Mr. Kurtz."

"I didn't do anything, Detective. I didn't take a dollar out of your casino. Why don't you chase down Alfie? He's the one who did the betting." He turned away, then mumbled, "Stupid kiss-ass."

"What's that about?"

"Nothing."

"You better talk to me, Mr. Kurtz. Or you're not going back to America anytime soon."

Kurtz took a deep breath.

"I need a smoke. Is that OK?"

LaPorta nodded. Kurtz pulled a pack of cigarettes from his shirt pocket. LaPorta resisted the urge to ask for one.

"Look, Detective, Alfie thinks he's my wife's protector, OK? He's more like her manservant. He's always around, always getting her every little thing she needs." He placed a cigarette between his lips. "Makes me look bad."

"Don't you mean your ex-wife?"

Kurtz pulled a lighter from his jacket. "Yeah. My ex-wife. So?"

"You broke up with her in college, right? Where you played soccer? Goalie? Why did you two get back together?"

Kurtz glared. "Where are you getting all this?"

"Oh, I know plenty about you, Mr. Kurtz."

The truth was, LaPorta only knew what Alfie had written in his notebook. But if it helped solve the case, he planned to use it.

"Now, one last time. How was Alfie Logan part of your scheme?"

Kurtz set his jaw. "I told you. I don't know what scheme you're talking about."

LaPorta rose from the table. "Have it your way. But you'll be staying here for a while."

He went to the door, then turned back.

"It must really piss you off though, huh?"

"What?"

"That Alfie won two million bucks betting the numbers you rigged."

Kurtz's eyes widened.

"Oh, that's right. You bolted before his last bet. He put all those chips down a third time, and hit a single play. Two million. Funny thing is, he sent it all to your ex."

Kurtz threw his head back. His neck muscles bulged.

"You sure you don't want to tell me how you two were connected?" LaPorta asked.

"For the last freaking time, I don't have anything to do with Alfie Logan!" Kurtz shouted. "I wish he was dead!"

THE QUEEN'S STAIRCASE

Gianna, wearing an oversized sweatshirt, walked quickly along Elizabeth Avenue, hands in her pockets, a hood pulled over her head. In the moonlight, she saw the dark outline of Fort Fincastle, built in the eighteenth century to protect the island from pirates. She saw its tall, cylindrical water tower nearby. The landmark staircase Alfie had mentioned was just below, surrounded by high walls. She glanced at her watch. It was nearly 11:30 p.m.

She had persuaded Detective LaPorta to let her return to her hotel, on the promise that she would remain there until tomorrow for further questioning. But an hour ago, she had slipped through the sliding doors of her room's private patio and snuck out through the resort's rear hedges.

She felt bad about lying. LaPorta had driven her back himself, firing endless questions about Alfie's story.

"He's suffering from delusions, Detective," Gianna kept saying. "You can't make sense of a sick mind."

Privately, she was less than sure. Yes, this whole invention of magical second chances was crazy. But so many early memories Alfie had written about *were* accurate. Why was the rest of it fantasy? Especially the parts about the two of them? They were never lovers. Clearly never husband and wife.

The truth was, when they graduated college, Gianna was headed to Patagonia to photograph wildlife, and she figured Alfie would pursue his music in New York. But, lacking any concrete plans, he asked if he could accompany her. "One last vacation," he had called it. He was a big help with the equipment on that trip and provided friendly conversation in the otherwise lonely hours away from home.

When Gianna sold the photos, the magazine that bought them offered her a new assignment in Glacier Bay, Alaska. She asked Alfie if he wanted to repeat his role. They continued on from there. The Galápagos. The archipelagos in Norway. The rain forest in Borneo. Several years passed. Gianna's reputation grew. She shared some of the money she was making with Alfie. And pretty soon, photography was her full-time job and Alfie was her full-time assistant.

They were good travel companions and enjoyed the easy dialogue of longtime friends. They laughed constantly. They finished each other's food. Over time, Gianna trusted Alfie with everything—her car, her house, her ATM card. She kept encouraging him to pursue his music, and he often said he would but never did.

When she met Mike again at her ten-year Boston University reunion, they rekindled their old romance. Alfie had been leery. When they got engaged, Alfie wouldn't look at her.

"Why do you hate him?" she asked.

"I don't hate him. I just don't want him to hurt you."

"He's not going to hurt me, Alfie."

"He did once."

And, of course, he did it again. Gianna put up with Mike for fourteen years, because she thought a marriage meant enduring, and they'd been pretty good at the beginning and she'd hoped they could start a family. But it didn't happen. Mike had a decent job in medical sales, then lost it because of his drinking. He lost another one when he cursed out his boss in front of a roomful of clients.

He turned to gambling. Casinos. Horse races. Gianna stuck by him. Even tried to find him a new firm. But when she discovered he'd secretly used her money to purchase a speedboat which he'd used to take a waitress on a three-day trip to Key West, she'd had enough.

Their divorce was long and ugly and, as the breadwinner, Gianna had to pay Mike alimony. He used the funds for gambling, while she downsized to a small property by the beach in South Carolina. Alfie moved into a guest house behind it. They'd lived there ever since.

Alfie was a sounding board for Gianna's gripes about Mike, work, or anything else. He handled her shooting schedule and her equipment. He fixed whatever was broken around the property. And, now that she thought about it, she *had* rested her head on his shoulder many times and cried on it often. But she had always taken that as friendship, not intimacy. Not romantic love. Never that. Or so she told herself.

Now, hurrying to meet a man she thought she knew so well, and realizing she didn't know him at all, she wasn't sure where one emotion ended and another began.

*

Alfie Logan sat on the bottom tread of the historic staircase, built by hand out of solid limestone. It was an astounding construction, the work of many enslaved people. The surrounding walls were nearly a hundred feet high and draped with vegetation. While the area was often crowded during tourist hours, it was dark and silent now, with only moonlight as illumination.

Alfie's heart was racing. *Would she come? Had she read the pages?* Although so much of his life was a rewind, this was all-new. He had no idea how the night would end, only that he would suffer a stroke at six minutes after midnight, according to his calculations. He hadn't allowed for much time with Gianna. That was deliberate. If she was open to hearing his confession, it wouldn't take long, and he could endure what came next with a certain peace of mind.

And if she didn't show up? Well, he didn't want a lot of time brooding while he waited for a blood vessel to burst in his brain.

"Alfie?"

And there she was, walking toward him, bathed in blue moonlight. The one true love of his life.

She lowered her sweatshirt hood, pushed two hands through her hair and smiled like she always did when she saw him, as he croaked the words, "Gianna. You came."

"Of course."

She sat down next to him. Her voice dropped. "Alfie? What's going on?"

He realized she now knew everything. The notebook had revealed a lifetime of secrets. *What's going on?* The question seemed too big to answer.

"Please, Alfie. You can tell me. Are you sick? Has something affected your . . . thinking?"

"My thinking is fine," he said softy.

"But what you wrote in that notebook—"

"It's true."

"Alfie."

"All of it."

Gianna placed her palms on the sides of his face. He inhaled with her touch.

"Oh, Alfie," she whispered. "You're not well."

"Don't feel bad for me, Gianna. I've been blessed. I got to be with the woman I loved for more than forty years."

Gianna raised her eyebrows.

"Me?"

"Of course."

"But we were never . . . in love."

"Speak for yourself."

He took her hands. They were cold, and he squeezed them together.

"Gianna, listen. When I was in the hospital, after my stroke, I felt like I had wasted my life. I missed you so much. I missed the way you greeted me when I came home, the little notes you left me on the piano, the touch of you in the morning, the way we used to make love."

Gianna felt dizzy.

"Alfie, that *never happened*."

"It did. Once. Sharing a bed with you was such a privilege.

Losing it left a hole inside me forever. But in that hospital room I realized, even if I could never receive such love again, I hadn't lost the ability to give it. To shower you with it from afar."

He smiled. "There's no rule against that."

Gianna looked down, but Alfie lifted a finger under her chin until her eyes again met his. "That's what I did, Gianna. As soon as I'd recovered enough to croak out a single syllable, I chose the one word that's defined my whole insane life."

"*Twice?*" she whispered.

"*Twice.* And I went all the way back to 1978, that day in Philadelphia, during the thunderstorm, remember? Only this time, knowing you could never care for me the same way, I never took that elephant necklace out of the bag. Never said 'I love you.' Never kissed you through the glass.

"We hung out, as friends, and from that point on, I did everything I could to stay close to you. I became your sounding board, your confidant, your lens-carrier, your midnight pizza-cutter..."

Gianna, despite herself, began to smile.

"Your runner-to-the-drugstore, your morning coffee-maker, your electrician, your caulker, your B12 shot-in-the-thigh-giver..."

She was laughing now.

"Your chauffer, your toilet-unclogger, your temperature-taker, your one-phone-call-away assistant—"

"My everything," Gianna whispered.

"Everything I could be, except the one thing I couldn't."

Gianna dropped her head. She saw their feet lined up together, her two white tennis shoes, his two brown loafers.

"You really believe this," she murmured.

"Why wouldn't I? It's the truth."

He waited until she looked up again.

"If you can't accept the stories of my many lives," he said, "just accept the message that runs through all of them."

"What message?"

"That you are deeply loved, Gianna. That you have always been deeply loved. That every night, sleeping in another room, I was dreaming of lying beside you. That for all these years, you've had my heart to break.

"And all that time, this second time around, I never left your side."

*

With that, Gianna broke down. She buried her face in her hands. She had stopped imagining any man's affection after things ended so badly with Mike. She'd hidden herself in work and flipped off the switch on intimacy. She felt tears filling the space between her palms and her cheeks. Were they for Alfie, or for herself?

"I'm going to have to leave now," Alfie whispered.

"Wait," she gasped. "Are you really dying?"

"Well, in a few minutes, I'm going to kind of lose it. I'll have a stroke. And I won't be able to speak. I don't know how much longer I'll last after that. I get the sense it's not long. It's OK. Like my grandmother said, there comes a point where you want to see what comes next more than you want to go back."

Gianna tried to imagine a life without Alfie. To her surprise, it hurt like a mule kick. She had not, until that moment, realized how much of her existence truly was wrapped around this man she had never married, had never slept with, had never kissed, yet who claimed to have memories of all those things. And what hurt the most was that the way he described those memories was better than any love she had actually experienced in her life.

She hooked her arm in his, and then, as she had done so many times before, curled against his chest and laid her head on his shoulder. Alfie inhaled the smell of her, rested his chin atop her hair, and gazed skyward. He thought to himself that he could die in this moment, it wouldn't be so bad.

*

"Gianna," Alfie suddenly whispered.

"Mmm?"

"Does LaPorta have the notebook?"

"I think so."

"That explains it."

He pulled away slightly and nodded up ahead. Gianna saw a flashing police car approaching.

"He must have read the ending," Alfie said. "When I told you to meet me here."

Gianna grabbed his shoulders.

"Alfie. You have to go."

"Where?"

"Go back in time!"

"What?"

"Jump. Whatever you do. Just get away from here!"

"I've done what I wanted to do, Gianna. You know everything now. There's no point in going backward anymore."

"There is a point! You'll escape this. You'll live. Don't you want to live?"

He placed his hands gently on hers. "I've lived a long time already."

"But *I* want you to live. I don't want to be in a world without you!"

Alfie smiled. "I want, and you want, and God does what God wants."

"ALFIE LOGAN! GIANNA RULE!"

LaPorta had exited the car and was sprinting down a pathway and screaming. "HEY! YOU STAY RIGHT THERE!"

"Alfie?" Gianna spun toward him. "Run!"

And because he would do anything she asked, he inhaled, took a final look, then broke free and hurried up the steps. To his surprise, Gianna was running behind him. Two steps. Six. Ten. Twenty.

"What are you doing?" he yelled.

"Take me with you!"

"What?"

"I want to go wherever you go!"

He stopped, panting.

"So you believe me, then?"

"Yes. I believe you."

He smiled. "That's all I wanted, Gianna."

She grabbed his face.

"No! Want more, Alfie!"

His gaze shot from Gianna to LaPorta, who had almost reached the bottom step. Alfie reached into his pocket, removed a crumpled envelope, and dropped it.

Then he took the hand of the woman he had silently loved for this lifetime and another lifetime and, in truth, from the day he met her, and they ran up a miracle of a staircase together with a detective chasing them in the moonlight.

Just before they reached the top, Gianna looked at Alfie and wished to herself that she could have her time with him all over again. She wished it more intensely than anything she had ever wished for in her life.

LaPorta tripped on a step, came down hard, slammed his knee, and cursed. He scrambled back up. But by the time he reached the top of the staircase, the suspects were gone.

Eight

NASSAU

LaPorta slumped in his chair and moved the ice pack around his knee. He grimaced. It was early morning in the police station, and he wanted a cup of coffee but couldn't easily get up. He cursed himself for not having more officers with him last night. It was stupid to race out there alone—which is what he'd done after reading the final pages of the notebook.

"Good morning, hero."

Sampson was walking toward his desk.

"You all right?"

"I'll be fine," LaPorta said. "Eventually."

Sampson smiled. "There's sixty-four steps in that staircase. For an old man, you did pretty good getting to the top."

"The people I was chasing were older than me."

"Yeah, that's sad."

"Any news on our guy?"

Sampson shook his head. "Still in the hospital. Can't move. Can't speak."

LaPorta had found Alfie Logan lying in the grass by an old shack near the fort, not far from the top of the staircase. He was unconscious. The doctors at Princess Margaret Hospital said he'd suffered a stroke, just as Alfie had predicted in his notebook. Every time he thought about that, it made LaPorta shiver.

"My officers found this," Sampson said.

He handed over a crumpled envelope. LaPorta blinked at the handwritten words on the outside.

"For Detective LaPorta, to be read upon my death."

"What the hell?" he mumbled.

"Yeah, Vincent," Sampson said. "What the hell?"

LaPorta took a deep breath. He moved the ice pack off his knee.

"Aren't you gonna read it?"

"Yeah, yeah. Give me a second."

LaPorta held still, staring at the envelope, trying to absorb the tumultuous rush of the last two days, the arrest, the hours with Alfie, the crazy notebook reading, the dealer, the croupier, interrogating Mike Kurtz, and the two million dollars sent to the mysterious Gianna Rule, who, as of this morning, still could not be found.

He ripped open the envelope and flattened the handwritten contents on his desk. He recognized the paper from a familiar notebook.

Dear Vincent–

I'm sorry to have to finish our conversation this way. By the time you read this, speech will not be an option. I pray this confession gets to you.

You will likely have spoken with Mike Kurtz by now, and if you are as good as I think, you will have learned about his plan to rig the roulette results. As you now know, he was not successful. Not in this existence.

But in a previous one, he was. In fact, he won a great deal of money on two straight bets. He might have gotten away with it, except the croupier got nervous with all the chips Mike was accumulating and tried to switch the ball back. Security noticed. They approached, and Mike ran from the table.

They chased him to the parking lot. They saw him speed away in a rental car. They pursued him in their van, weaving through traffic, until a half mile away, he spun out at a light and crashed into another vehicle, crushing the legs of the driver, an innocent casino employee who was heading into work.

I had to jump back in time to stop all of this. For one thing, Mike is a louse, but Gianna once loved him, at least in a fashion. I didn't want her heart broken by him rotting in a Bahamian prison. And, as he owns a part of her photography operation, his criminality would surely reflect on her business. She doesn't deserve that.

But there is a second reason I went back, one you might be more interested in:

That employee, the one who had his legs crushed in Mike's futile escape, was an important member of the casino security team. An American.

Detective Vincent LaPorta.

I didn't want you to suffer that way.

*

This leaves only my part in the roulette scam to explain. After all that you have gone through on this case—what you remember and what you cannot—you deserve answers.

Here is what happened. Having seen what numbers Mike bet the first time around, I used one of my second chances to go back a day, then gathered all the money I could. I went to the table just before Mike and his men were about to make their move. Mike saw me and snapped, "What the hell are you doing here, Alfie?" That was good. I had him nervous.

Then I slapped my chips on the first number before his man could. I saw them looking at each other. Mike shook his head no and his man never made his bet.

I won, then immediately placed all my winnings on their second number. I could see Mike fuming. His guys were confused.

When I won again, he motioned them to walk away.

They departed—and so did Mike—having committed no crime but the phony ball. Given that, I am hoping you can be lenient, Vincent. After all, you have been spared years of pain and rehabilitation, even if you are unaware of it. One favor merits another, I hope.

Now, to the final bet. I told you that I did not cheat to win the two million dollars. And I did not. I wanted no part of the chips I had amassed in stopping Mike, nearly $58,000. So I impulsively pushed them all onto

28 black. I chose that number because Gianna's birthday is the second of August. I figured, why not? It's as good a way to lose as any other.

Except the number won.

I know. It's crazy. The first thing in decades that I left to total chance, and it came up a jackpot.

There's a lesson there, I think.

So I sent the money to Gianna. My final act of loyal assistance. I will be dead soon, and unable to help her anymore. If you contact my attorney, you will find that I left everything to her in my will anyhow.

With the exception of the two hundred thousand I sent to Africa.

And you're probably not going to love this last part.

I found out Juma had sold Lallu for a high price to a recreation outfit in Zimbabwe. They were chaining her in a pen and making her give rides to tourists. It hurt my soul. That's not a life.

So I bought her freedom. I arranged for her to be taken home to Kenya. Because I won't be able to do this myself, I put your name on the paperwork.

Technically, Vincent, you now own an elephant.

At the bottom of this page is a confirmation number for two tickets to Zimbabwe. First class. And full instructions. I know it's asking a lot, but after all the time we spent together today (and I repeated many parts of our interrogation so I could get to know you better) I sense that deep down you are a good man, if a flawed one, like me. And that you will help. Let Lallu die in freedom, as I wish to die myself.

I believe you'll find a way.

I hope you continue to catch the bad guys, Vincent, and you find contentment. And love, if you are lucky. What I've learned—after all this time—is that love is indeed the only rational act.

And the only real lifesaver.

Unlike those ones you pop in your mouth.

*Warmest regards,
Alfred "Alfie" Logan*

*

Nine days later, LaPorta exited the hospital's sliding doors and squinted against the sunlight. It always felt strange to leave a building where someone had just died and suddenly be in sunshine, wind tickling your face. Did the world forget us so quickly? Or did it never take much notice in the first place?

LaPorta never got to question Alfie further. His speech improved only enough for a few grunts. Then, two days ago, he developed sepsis. His weakened body couldn't fight it off. He died just before sunrise.

LaPorta reached for his car keys and felt Alfie's final letter in his pocket. He pulled it free and studied the last handwritten paragraphs. Then, as often happens after someone you know dies, he thought about his own mortality. His age. His health. His life.

And his wife.

He took out his phone and called her.

"Hey," she said.

"Hey."

"It's kind of early. Everything all right?"

"Yeah." LaPorta sighed. "I've been thinking. You want to get away? Take a trip? Just the two of us?"

"Yes." Her voice perked up. "Yes, Vince. I'd love that."

"Good."

"Do you have someplace in mind?"

He paused.

"How about Africa?"

Epilogue

August 1978

They were calling it "the storm of the year." All along Market Street in the city of Philadelphia, the rain blew sideways and the wind gusted near hurricane force.

In the middle of this chaos, a woman suddenly appeared, young, not yet twenty years old. Her thick hair, the color of coal, blew wildly around her face, covering her eyes. She seemed confused, as if this storm were a surprise.

She clutched her handbag and quickly undid the clasp as the rain soaked her jeans and matted them against her legs.

Then Gianna Rule took out her wallet, flipped it open, and stared at the photo on her driver's license. It was from Boston, where she'd lived when she was in college.

So this is what it's like, she thought to herself. *You relive everything. Just how Alfie described it.*

Looking up, she spotted the front entrance of Gimbels department store. She narrowed her gaze at the sight of a revolving door, and Alfie at the window, waving his arms.

She was immediately struck at how youthful he looked, and she wondered if she looked the same. She squeezed her upper thigh. Thinner. She grabbed her waist. Smaller. She lifted her handbag over her head against the rain and hurried across the street with a surprising quickness, her sneakers splashing up rainwater.

And in those steps, Gianna's fear turned to joy, and her regret to hope. When she pushed through the revolving doors, she knew they would jam. When she laughed and said, "Oh, God, Alfie, why do I hang out with you?" she knew he would say, "Because I'm fun!"

And when she slid close to the dirty glass that separated them, she knew that in this world, he would choose to keep his feelings hidden. Because he believed that she could never love him.

But this was *her* rewind. She could decide where her heart went. So she leaned in toward the man who had loved her like no other. And while she wasn't sure how she had inherited his power, except to think his death had passed it on to her, it didn't matter. If this was a dream, she knew what she wanted. And if this was reality, she wanted the same thing.

"What's in the bag, Alfie?" she said.

"Nothing special."

"You sure?"

"It was just an idea I had. It was probably stupid."

Gianna took a long, deep breath, as if resetting every cell in her body.

"Try me," she whispered.

She watched Alfie remove a small silver elephant on a chain. She felt tears welling in her eyes. She beckoned him closer. And as they kissed through the dirty glass, she felt something old yet new explode in her heart. Because The Truth About True Love is that it can wait a lifetime. Or two.

THE END

From the Author

As this is a love story, I should begin my thanks with those I love the most, and that means Janine, our darling Nadie, my brother and sister, Peter and Cara, my relatives, my in-laws, my dear friends, and my very large Haitian family, all of whom have given me immeasurable joy and a home for my heart. They say it's hard to write a book about love if you haven't known much of it. By that measure, I should have many more such books in me.

Alfie is fictional, but much of his love life was based on incidents or people in mine. I never snuck into a lion's cage, but I did spill chocolate milk all over a cute girl once, and I did have an awkward sixth-grade make-out experience in a closet. For all those early crushes who shaped my heart, even through embarrassment, I thank you.

With regard to this specific story, gratitude goes to my editor, Karen Rinaldi, who, when I first described *Twice*, gave one of those "Oooh, I just got goose bumps" reactions, which is how I know I am on the right track. And my longtime friend and agent, David Black, who was so patient in getting to read it—"I'm here when you're ready"—yet so encouraging once he had.

My early readers, Ali, Jesse, Rosey, and Kim, kept asking me for "more pages!," which is what you need to hear when you are eyeballs-deep in the process. Several of our kids from Haiti also gave it the once-over and a thumbs up, which meant a lot.

Steve Bourie, author of the *American Casino Guide*, was helpful in understanding the inner workings of the casino gambling world, and roulette. And a trip to the Bahamas certainly helped. The Queens Staircase is real and majestic and a perfect place for a final scene of any love story.

To the folks at HarperCollins, as always, my deep appreciation for your belief in my work: Brian Murray, Jonathan Burnham, Leslie Cohen, Tina Andreadis, Doug Jones, Leah Wasielewski, Tom Hopke, Kirby Sandmeyer, and Milan Bozic, who took a sketch idea I had and came up with this beautiful cover in a heartbeat.

The team at Black, Inc. is endlessly supportive: Susan Raihofer, who brings my stories to the world, Anagha Purevu, Anna Zinchuk, and Nell Beck. Thank you all.

My circle of support helps make all my books possible: Kerri Alexander, who proofreads my proofreading; Jo-Ann Barnas, a wonderful writer herself who shoulders my research; Antonella Iannarino, who drags me lovingly into the world of social media; and Vince Cracchiolo, who handles all things tech. And Mendel is still a bum.

Nothing in this world happens without God, and I am humbled more and more by the grace and blessings God has given me in this life. I believe strongly in charity, and several people made donations to help needy folks in exchange for seeing their names appear in these pages. So Linda Kay, Andrew Berry, Colleen and Kent Klausner, and Kim and Jim Varga, thank you for your kindness.

And, finally, of course, my thanks to you, loyal readers, semi-loyal readers, first-time readers, and folks who picked this book up by accident. I am deeply grateful you came along for the ride.

Authors get a lot of questions. One that I've heard and, after this book, am bound to hear more of is this: "Would you do anything differently if you had the chance?"

Yes, I would. In fact, I can think of twenty things right now. But ask me if I'd trade how I'd changed as a result of my mistakes, and my answer would be different. It's like Yaya said. If you keep getting second chances, you won't learn a damn thing. I've learned a lot. The older I get, the more precious those lessons become.

I am so grateful for this life that keeps on teaching.

Mitch Albom
Detroit, MI
May 2025

About the Author

Mitch Albom is the author of numerous books of fiction and nonfiction, which have collectively sold forty-two million copies in forty-eight languages worldwide. He has written eight number one *New York Times* bestsellers, including *Tuesdays with Morrie*, the bestselling memoir of all time; award-winning television films; stage plays; screenplays; a nationally syndicated newspaper column; and a musical. Through his work at the *Detroit Free Press*, he was inducted into both the National Sports Media Association and Michigan Sports halls of fame and is the recipient of the 2010 Red Smith Award for lifetime achievement. He founded the nonprofit SAY Detroit, which provides pathways to success for Detroiters in need through major health, housing, and education initiatives. He also founded a dessert shop and a gourmet popcorn line to help fund it. Albom operates Have Faith Haiti, a home and school for impoverished children and orphans in Port-au-Prince, which he visits monthly. He lives with his wife, Janine, in Michigan.